SILENT PARTNER

A California Police K9 Story

Jennifer Chase

PUBLISHED BY:
JEC PRESS

ISBN: 978-0-9829536-0-0

PRINTED IN THE UNITED STATES OF AMERICA

Praise for SILENT PARTNER

Won SILVER Medal Award for Suspense &
FINALIST for Thriller from International Book Awards Readers'
Favorite

*"Silent Partner is definitely a must read and an outstanding novel
up there with Clancy and Baldacci."*
Fran Lewis, Reviewer

*"Silent Partner is a fast paced thriller that will keep the reader on
the edge of their seat till they reach the amazing conclusion of the
book."*
Readers Favorite

"Silent Partner is highly riveting and full of nonstop action."
Midwest Book Review

*"The emotional heart of this book comes from the mutual love
that exists between the humans and their dogs."*
Amazon Review

*"In the world of police procedurals this book stands out as being
unique and well written."*
Amazon Review

*"A thought provoking read that mines the psychological depths of
policing and the depravity of a psychopath."*
Amazon Review

*Psychological thriller that integrates the bond between man and
dog."*
Writers in the Sky

*"This is a fabulous detective driven thriller that I highly
recommend!"*
Amazon Review

More books by Jennifer Chase

Award Winning Emily Stone Thriller Series:

Compulsion
Dead Game
Dark Mind
Dead Burn
Dark Pursuit
Dead Cold

Chip Palmer Forensics Mysteries:

Body of the Crime
Scene of the Crime

California K9 Series:

Silent Partner
Loyal Partner

Short Stories:

Never Forgotten
First Watch

Non-Fiction:

How to Write a Screenplay

Visit her at:

www.authorjenniferchase.com

"The dog represents all that is best in man."

- Etienne Charlet

"The dog is the most faithful of animals and would be much esteemed were it not so common. Our Lord God has made his greatest gift the commonest."

- Martin Luther

"A righteous man cares for the needs of his animal, but the kindest acts of the wicked are cruel."

- Proverbs 12:10

"I care not for a man's religion whose dog and cat are not the better for it."

- Abraham Lincoln

For all the working and retired K9 Units

SILENT PARTNER

FOREWARD

Being a police officer is a job like no other. Dealing with negativity on an ongoing basis can really wear on ones psyche. In general, the normal police officer works alone or in some agencies in two officer units. There is one division within the Police Department that has an officer and a partner.

This partner is unlike any other partner in the Police Department. The officer working with this partner takes his partner home with him at night. The partner becomes part of the officer's family. I'm not talking about a human partner, I'm talking about a canine partner or K9 for short. I had the opportunity and pleasure to have worked in the K-9 unit for 8 years during my 28-year career.

I found working K9 to be one of the most challenging and yet rewarding times of my career. You see, working with a dog partner is so different from working with a human partner. Your day doesn't end when your shift ends. When you get off work, you don't leave your equipment behind. You take your partner home with you and the shift continues. The dog needs to be fed and watered. After he is done eating then you take him for a walk before hitting the sack. In the morning, another walk with my partner, and then my morning coffee, and maybe a treat for him before going to work.

Training is not just something you do when at work. I would train with my dogs constantly. Not necessarily police type training, like search and protection work, but also obedience and obstacle training. Our walks would be off the beaten path locations so that we would have to climb rocks, go over downed trees, through tunnels or whatever I would come across. As for the obedience training, not only did I want my dog to chase down the bad guy or protect me when I was in danger, but I wanted him to be a good member of the community I lived in. I wanted kids to be able to pet him and other dogs to interact with him without the fear of him causing a problem. Thankfully, the dogs I worked during my career were great dogs and easily some of the best dogs I ever owned.

In my career, I was fortunate enough to have worked two dogs. Rommel my first partner was a big German shepherd. We got him from a couple that was moving into an apartment and could not have a dog there. He was the first dog in the department's history and he was my partner. We worked together for almost 5 years before he became ill and couldn't survive his illness. The hardest thing I ever had to do was say goodbye to him. I felt like not only was I losing my partner at work, but I was losing a family member. I cried a lot of tears that day. And I drank—a lot. The officers in my department were super supportive. They rallied around me the day he died and I saw how much they respected him.

Thankfully, the department saw fit to allow me to have another dog and that's when I got Iso. He was a smaller German shepherd, but a real fireball when it came to working. Both Rommel and Iso loved to work. The best feeling for a K9 officer is when you deploy your dog for the first time and he finds the bad guy. The countless hours of training all seemed worth it at that time.

It's not an easy job working K9. It can be very frustrating, but mostly it was a very rewarding experience. Later on in my career, I was assigned as the K9 supervisor after I was promoted to sergeant. I was able to mentor younger K9 officers and watch them grow into good working dog teams. I required a lot out of these officers and their dogs, but in the end, I felt we had some of the best dog teams in the area.

As I said earlier, the most rewarding time of my career was the time I spent working K9. Having a loving protective partner with me every day in the patrol car, not only made me feel safe, but was also a lot of fun. We had so many adventures that I could easily write a book about them. But in the end, I would not have traded my time in the K-9 unit for any other assignment in the Police Department. I always knew that no matter how bad my workday was going, when I got back to my car, my dog would be there happy to see me and ready to go out and find another bad guy.

In the book SILENT PARTNER, Jennifer Chase, the author and my friend, has captured the spirit and essence of what it's like to work with a dog as your partner. As I read the book, I flashed back many times to situations I've dealt with as a K9 Handler. Some of the flashbacks were not the best, but in the end, we caught the bad guy and she has helped me to relive one of the best times of my career. If you want a great read and a feel for what working K9 is like then SILENT PARTNER is it.

Mark Keyes
Police Sergeant - K9 Handler/Supervisor
Daly City Police Department
(Retired)

SILENT PARTNER

PROLOGUE
1969

The rain had finally stopped on the twenty-sixth consecutive day of downpours. It was only a brief reprieve. An intense humidity reeked from the undergrowth of the dense, twisted jungle foliage and heavily saturated earth.

The heavy air made it difficult to breathe as the men trudged onward. The sticky uniforms that clung to the bodies of the weary soldiers were a constant reminder of the unbearable weather, while happier memories of being home in the United States were constantly on their minds.

The soldiers of the U.S. Army Platoon of the 26th Infantry found themselves deep inside the jungles of Vietnam fighting a war they didn't completely understand. Many of the men were barely eighteen years old and still lived at home with their parents in small towns in places like Iowa, Delaware, and Indiana. With moderate stealth, they continued to trudge onward through the overgrown vegetation.

Carrying his M16 rifle poised, and eyeing every possible moving shadow around him that might resemble the enemy, Alec Weaver walked in his point position as a combat tracker, looking for rogue enemy assassins. It wasn't the choice spot for any soldier, but it was different for him and he didn't mind it. He knew that he was safe as he looked down at Max.

With his ears perked and alert and head low, a regal German shepherd dutifully guided the men, his keen dog senses picking up everything around them as he trailed a thick tail against a lean eighty-five pound body. The humidity didn't seem to be a problem for the canine. He was oblivious to the discomforts of the jungle because he had a job to do and he knew how to do it well.

Alec's combat tracking team consisted of five men, including himself, and he was the dog handler. Butch, the combat's team leader, had most of the experience in the group, even though he was only two years older than the rest of the team. He was from a tiny town in Indiana that most had never heard of in casual conversation. Tom, the cover man, was an expert in weapons, but a man of few words. Brett, the visual tracker, was the jokester of the group, providing the platoon with comic relief when necessary, but he definitely knew his stuff when it came to tracking. Terry was the RTO, or radio-telephone operator, and was probably the most conservative and the most educated of the group with three semesters of college under his belt. He wanted to become a lawyer and if he survived the jungles in Vietnam, there would be no doubt that he would succeed.

Alec had spent several months training with Max in obedience school and then went on to the combat tracker dog handler course, where he had been hand-picked to be a handler from a list of volunteers. He had grown up with dogs at home in Los Angeles, but he had never trained in the capacity that he now found himself. He knew exactly how to read the dog; every little twitch, hesitation, and snaps of the head were clear signals to him. These dogs were trained to detect trip wires, snipers, and any type of booby traps set to kill enemy soldiers by the most hideous means.

Max was an exceptional dog, intelligent and the most loyal best friend anyone could ask for in the current foreign nightmare, an unbearable nightmare that had gone on long enough. Still, there was a job to be done. Having Max at his side made it a little more bearable for Alec who was only days away from his nineteenth birthday. At least he had hoped that he would live to see another birthday. Alec remembered the motto that was ingrained in him from superiors and trainers: *train hard, fight easy*.

Max stopped.

He stared straight ahead.

The dog didn't move his position, his head was held high and his breathing turned shallow.

Waiting.

Deducing what was up ahead and what it meant to their immediate safety.

To pass the time, Alec had been accessing happy childhood memories and almost stepped on Max's hind feet. He abruptly stopped and read the dog. He raised his hand to alert the rest of the platoon to stop.

Everyone halted in their tracks.

It was eerily quiet, too quiet.

The men scanned the jungle all around expecting the worst and asking themselves silently who would be the next fatality. A couple of the men actually twitched with agonizing anticipation.

The vines and overgrown leaves dripping with moisture seemed to slowly close in on them—nature's subtle way of alerting them that something wasn't where it was supposed to be at the moment.

Max's right ear twitched backward, assessing any subtle sound.

Alec felt a chill as goosebumps appeared on his arms, and cold perspiration rolled down the back of his neck.

In the silence, the tension rose throughout the group.

In slow motion, Max sat down and kept his gaze forward. He was firmly planted and it was obvious that he wasn't going to move.

Alec knew too well what Max had caught wind of, and he moved cautiously until he spotted the trip wire that had been cleverly concealed in the jungle vines. He had seen what this type of booby trap could do to a man. In an instant, limbs and other body pieces were savagely torn apart, leaving behind a bloody mass of gristle that had once been a living, breathing human being. The only good aspect was that death was instantaneous, at least most of the time, but it alerted the enemy that there were more possible casualties to be had.

Alec gestured to the others, indicating the trip wire, one of many they had encountered over the past several months. Max stood and crept closer to the wire and stepped over it. The men followed the same action and continued their trek through the jungle.

A twig snapped.

Max barked ferociously, looking upward.

Alec swung his weapon toward the faint noise and spotted an enemy sniper huddled in a tree. He opened fire, riddling bullets through the trees, almost cutting that part of the forest in half. In unison, several other soldiers fired at the tree. The enemy soldier fell to the ground with a thud, never moving again.

Max quickly went back to his point position and continued to lead the group deeper into the dense jungles of Vietnam. There were more enemy soldiers—waiting for them.

1983

Jack Davis pumped his skinny eight-year-old legs faster as his bike zoomed down a dirt road just before the O'Connells' rundown farm. It was summer and nothing could stand in his way to be outside, free from chores, and at his favorite fishing hole with his best friend. It was the greatest time of the year.

School was something in the past and not even a slight thought for the near future. His best friend, Pete, was meeting him at their secret spot with some new glowworms that he had confiscated from his older brother.

Two police cars followed by a tan four-door car sped past Jack with their lights flashing, no sirens.

Jack pulled his bike over to the side of the road next to a broken fence and watched as the emergency vehicles turned down the O'Connells' long dirt driveway. Dust plumes filled the air with a massive beige cloud making it difficult to see the farmhouse. Less than two minutes later, a white van traveling at a much slower speed followed the previous cars and disappeared down the driveway.

It was obvious that something terrible had happened. Jack had heard stories at school about the monster who lived at the O'Connell farm. At least that's what the kids called him, but in reality Mr. O'Connell was a bad man and his wife and two daughters suffered the most from it.

When he was sure that there weren't any more police vehicles racing to the farm, Jack squeezed through the broken fence, pushing his bike, and then eased down toward the commotion. He jumped back on the bike and coasted slowly down the hill. The bumpy back road jarred his bones, but his strong curiosity as well as concern seemed to get the better of him.

Jack watched as two sheriff's deputies roughly escorted Mr. O'Connell from the house, his arms behind his back, wrists secured in handcuffs, and his head hanging forward as he stared at the ground. He was barefoot and dressed in a grubby white t-shirt and blue jeans. It looked like he hadn't shaved or bathed in a week as his greasy dark brown hair was matted against the back of his skull.

The deputy's faces were grim as they put the man in the backseat of the patrol car and slammed the door shut.

Jack slowly rolled his bike as close as he dared. His first thought was that of the two sisters, Teresa who was eight and in his class, and Megan who had just turned five. He had taken them fishing several times.

Where are they?

Are they okay?

He expected to see Mrs. O'Connell any moment, but she never emerged through the front door. She was always nice to Jack and the other children, but she remained quiet most of the time.

A tall, dark-haired woman finally led the two little girls from the house to her car. Jack was somewhat relieved to see that the girls were okay, but no sight of their mom. The woman took a few minutes to secure the girls safely in the back seat of the car.

Jack found himself pulled by an imaginary force toward the scene to see what had happened. He didn't know exactly why, but he just had to know. Call it intense curiosity, but he also felt a need to protect his friends from harm. That was a big burden for any eight-year-old to carry. He remembered hearing that the girls had rich grandparents somewhere in California and he thought maybe they would go live with them.

He slowed his bike next to the tan car, planting his feet firmly on the ground. Teresa stared straight ahead and didn't show any expression or movement; she appeared to be in a trance. Megan slowly turned her petite face to look at Jack, her intense dark eyes seemingly searching his face for some type of explanation.

Jack froze, his eyes remaining locked on Megan's intense stare. One of the deputies saw him next to the car and told him to leave. For the first time, Jack looked inside the main entrance of the farmhouse and saw a plain white sheet spotted with bright red smears covering a body. There was blood splattered on the walls mixed with chunks of stuff. It was the most grisly thing that Jack had ever seen in his young life. He could barely comprehend what he was seeing, but it stirred something deep within him.

Something had awakened.

Jack didn't realize at the time that the experience would be forever imprinted in his mind and shape some of the choices he would make later in his life.

A deputy took hold of Jack's arm and gently steered him away from the scene. Jack kept his eyes on Megan as she watched him leave the farm. He felt his heart weigh heavy on his little chest. He wanted to help her, but there was nothing that he could do. He could only imagine what she was going through and how it had changed everything she knew up to this point about life and the people that you were supposed to trust.

CHAPTER ONE

Current day...

It was dark.

It was cold.

It was completely quiet.

With no windows or doors, escape was futile. There was a distinct smell of disinfectant along with a hint of mold that attacked the senses. It made it difficult to breathe and stale air trapped inside the lungs without anywhere else to go.

The waiting game was only putting off the inevitable.

Death.

She shifted her weight a couple of inches from her left side, but the duct tape pulled on her tender skin around her wrists, ankles, and across her mouth. Pieces of her hair were caught in the tape around her mouth and face. It stung her scalp with every movement she made.

The darkness around her felt like she was suspended in space a million miles from civilization.

She vaguely remembered the events of the evening. It had started out like any other night before she met her prospective clients for quick sex, and then she couldn't remember how she had ended up here. Her life had been tough at home, so she'd decided that she needed to take control of her own life. She'd left home a month ago and hadn't thought about it since—until now.

She missed her mom's overprotective attitude and her dad's persistent nagging of which college she needed to attend if she wanted to make something of herself. She never knew how much she would miss their company and how much she really loved them. She also didn't know how she could have so easily been turned out into the prostitution world without even realizing what had happened until it was too late.

She heard a sound like someone moving around above her. She tried to crane her neck to see any movement or light from her position, but only managed to cause herself more pain in the tight confinements of what was ultimately going to be her tomb.

Maybe someone has found me or seen what happened?

Maybe the police are searching for me right now?

She knew that wasn't the case, but tried desperately to keep positive thoughts in her last moments on earth. It was going to be her eighteenth birthday the following week. A tear rolled down her cheek. She wondered if her parents would still celebrate her birthdays after she was gone.

There was a noise again. It sounded like a metal object scraping on a cement floor. She could feel her heart rate increase, which made it even more difficult to breathe. Her arms and legs felt suddenly warm and clammy in the last ditch effort to move oxygen through the body. She knew that if she wasn't freed from her prison, the air supply would run out.

Faint footsteps approached, sounding like the person wore rubble-soled shoes. Then the sound of a latch being unlocked. Suddenly, the bright light blinded her. She couldn't see a thing, except a burning intensity making her eyes instantly water. She kept her eyes closed, but the forceful light still invaded through her eyelids. Slowly, the daylight began to darken and the room came into view.

A backlit figure stood over her, appearing more like an apparition than a real, living, breathing person.

No words were exchanged.

No plea expressed.

No threats given.

A searing pain impacted her stomach, followed by several more near her ribcage. She realized she was being stabbed repeatedly and couldn't escape her ultimate fate. She had to endure the torture. The pain increased exponentially to where she couldn't breathe as her lungs filled with blood. She felt like she was drowning and the world slowly faded away—the pain was gone.

The person slammed the large toolbox shut leaving a grisly surprise for the construction crew that came to work the next day.

CHAPTER TWO

The city streets were quiet. It was approaching 1 a.m. and most residents were fast asleep waiting for the next day to begin. The sleeping neighborhoods were completely unaware of who and what roamed the streets in the middle of the night.

Everyone had a story to tell and those people out in the middle of the night were no different. What made it unlike any other night was that there was a serial killer on the loose and it didn't seem like the police were close to catching him anytime soon. The erratic murders didn't seem to have any type of connection except for the victims it left behind.

The sidewalks, along with a few parked cars, were wet from a mild rain from a couple of hours ago. Large droplets of water on the road reflected the approaching headlights of a police cruiser.

The car idled as it slowed near quick flashes of light. In the shadows, transients were lighting up their scrounged cigarette butts in between quick swigs of cheap booze disguised in brown paper bags.

The cruiser paused for just a moment, then slowly moved on.

Deputy Jack Davis surveyed the streets with intense, dark blue eyes, casually running his fingers through his dark military haircut, looking for anything suspicious or out of place. His well-seasoned cop instincts from the past ten years rarely failed him.

Jack had many things weighing heavy on his mind. One of those things he was going to have out right now.

He vented to his partner, "You're such an adrenaline junkie. The end doesn't justify the means."

He sighed and continued, "I can't even look at you right now. You have to start following procedures otherwise Sarge is going to have both our asses on suspension."

It remained quiet inside the cruiser.

Jack finally spoke again. "Just because you sleep with me doesn't make this any easier. Do you have anything to say for yourself?"

A muscular one-hundred-pound black Labrador Retriever stared at his partner from the back seat. His large square head tilted slightly to one side, his black eyes fixed at attention as he watched his handler with building curiosity.

Jack demanded. "Say something. *Anything.*"

The dog barked twice and stood up, pushing his wet canine nose toward Jack and giving him a sloppy kiss on the side of his face, not forgetting the inside of his ear.

Jack smiled. For a brief moment, his tension melted away. "Like I can stay mad at you."

Jack roughly scratched the big dog's ears. He was rewarded with snorts and happy low-pitched whines.

The police cruiser took a turn down an alley between two closed businesses, their interiors lit only by low emergency lighting illuminating a shadowy glow from the display shelves.

Jack cut the engine but kept the car lights shining so he could see down the long alley. There were several dumpsters behind the electronics store and deli. The light bounced peculiar shadows and distorted views from the sides of the buildings and off barred security windows.

Jack's military boots hit the pavement as he got out of the car with purpose. He walked around the cruiser to the trunk, popped it open, and pulled out three gray blankets. He slammed the trunk closed, tucked the blankets under his right arm, and walked around the car.

With eyes focused and ears perked up, his four-legged partner never missed a single step or movement that Jack made. The dog's black eyes gave the canine an almost demonic appearance.

A sign posted on the side of the back window of the police car read boldly: CAUTION POLICE DOG—KENO. *Monterey County Sheriff* was printed down the side of the front doors.

Jack's squeaky gun belt echoed in unison with his footsteps while he walked down the alley as a few suspicious eyes peered out at him from the deep shadows.

Trash and flattened cardboard boxes littered the ground next to broken bottles that had been neatly swept against the side of the building. Some care had been taken to keep the glass from causing any injury to those who had to sleep there.

Upon closer inspection, Jack could see several homeless people hidden beneath the city's refuse cloaked in several layers of clothing with a few precious personal belongings clutched at their sides.

A young woman barely in her twenties with short blonde hair and a five-year-old child huddled together in their filthy clothing, shivering slightly from the damp evening. The local homeless shelter had only a few beds even for women and children. When they were already occupied, there was nothing else that they could do but find the safest place to hide out for the night. For them, this was the next safest place to be—away from the usual areas of downtown and under the bridge. It was cold, but they would be safe for another night.

Jack slowed his pace and with careful discretion he unfolded the blankets and gently wrapped them around the woman and little girl. They didn't say a word to him, but their eyes conveyed gratitude. It was difficult for Jack to just leave the homeless behind to shiver in the night, but he turned and kept his focus on the cruiser as he walked back.

Jack didn't raise his eyes to look through the windshield until he was seated back inside his warm cruiser. Several sets of eyes reflected from the harsh headlights, but they seemed to be more curious than wary of his presence. Some nameless faces had seen him before, especially on extreme cold nights and holidays. He resembled a dark knight coming to the aid of his homeless kingdom.

The cruiser slowly backed up and then disappeared into the night. The lights flashed like ghostly shadows for two seconds and then vanished as quickly as they had appeared. Once again, the alley was dark, quiet, and cold.

CHAPTER THREE

A dozen white pillar candles flickered in harmony off the stark white walls in the spacious bathroom. The flaming decorations were lined up at attention along the rim of the deep sunken bathtub, which had been carefully filled to the top with water.

The lulling fragrance of jasmine imbued the senses making it difficult not to breathe deeply and feel some enduring relaxation. Steam dissipated in the room, lingering for a few seconds before conforming to fixtures, walls, and finally the ornately decorated mirror.

The long vanity was covered with a large white towel. Three prescription bottles were lying on their sides and pills were scattered everywhere, some on the towel and more sprinkled and scattered around the counter. The bottles, containing a variety of anti-anxiety and depression medications from Clonazepam to Adapin and Paxil, were for a variety of ailments, and each were guaranteed to work, but none seemed to fully take care of the constant anxiety and the bottomless depression that followed soon after.

The feelings and thoughts of wild adventures and death she conjured in her mind were almost too much to bear at times. It seemed her moods would go from high energy that would allow her to be productive to low, depressing moods where she couldn't focus and didn't want to leave the safety of her own home. There were times, like this particular evening, that she wanted it all to stop permanently. She had suffered enough. Death seemed to be the only way for it all to stop forever. The only other idea that lingered in her thoughts was, could she do it?

A shiny dagger with a long, double-edged blade rested on the white towel glittering in the dim light. It appeared to be waiting for an important assignment that would finally take care of the constant pain and suffering. She'd shopped for the perfect knife that looked more like a movie prop than an actual weapon that would be in someone's collection.

A petite hand with long slender fingers wiped away a small circle in the mirror and revealed a young woman in her early thirties. Her shoulder length blonde hair rested against her neck, wet from her long bath. She stared at her reflection for a long time, looking deep into her dark brown eyes that seemed to subtly change from sadness to intense curiosity, but ultimately back to absolute misery. Her eyes would change color from brown to green and back again.

Her flowered silk robe hung loosely around her lean body, barely draped around her breasts. She closed her eyes, willing her memory to change her current condition. She relived the horror of murder repeatedly in her mind from when she was a child.

Nightmares of all proportion continued to haunt her both in her dreams at night and during her days. She felt the impending doom of life nip at her heels, fearing it would ultimately catch up to her and snuff out her existence.

She opened her eyes and stared at her reflection. Megan O'Connell had sat in this exact position and wondered the same things so many nights before.

Would this night be any different?

She must make a life or death decision. Somehow, she always seemed to manage to find something worth living for—no matter how small. She concluded that it was part of the human genetic makeup to find things worth living for. As usual, tears began to flow freely down her face. Her eyes looked like a muddied pond of dark despair. She popped a couple of pills into her mouth and swallowed them without water. It would only take about twenty minutes for her to feel the relief—even for just a while. She waited, and stared at her own changing reflection as it morphed into different people.

CHAPTER FOUR

In the still of the night, a primer gray late model 1990s Dodge van backed into the alley behind the popular restaurant and bar, then cut the engine. Both front passenger doors swung open and two men got out with purpose and crime on their minds. They looked up and down the alley to make sure no one had followed them to their rendezvous spot. The one heavyset man slammed the front door shut, followed closely by a tall, lanky and somewhat timid younger man.

Everything remained quiet and right on schedule.

A smoldering ember from the end of a generic cigarette was the only light in the alley. Within the shadows, a man dressed completely in black, sporting a perfectly trimmed goatee and mustache, approached the two men. He stood up straight from leaning against the brick, graffiti-tagged wall with an air of prison experience written all over him. Several amateur tattoos of gothic and satanic symbols were inked on the side of his neck, and they seemed to run down his arms to the backs of his hands in an eerie presentation. He took one last puff of his almost nonexistent butt and tossed it on the ground.

The heavyset man nodded in recognition and said, "Darrell."

Darrell let out a puff of smoke from his discarded cigarette. "Don, Johnny, nice to see you boys on time for once." He unzipped his black leather jacket and revealed a 9mm handgun tucked in his waistband. The distinct impression of alpha male dominated his character and he commanded respect. It was obvious who was in charge.

Johnny slid open the side of the van and retrieved two Smith & Wesson guns along with plenty of backup ammo. He seemed unsure of the scenario that was going to take place, but showed his confidence return when he handled the weapons. His greasy, blond hair looked shiny in the dim outdoor light. He moved his long, thin fingers over the weapons like an experienced pianist before a concert, secured one in his pocket and the other firmly in his right hand ready for action.

Don followed similar suit and took out a crowbar and shotgun from the other side of the van as his preferred weapons of choice. His demeanor was different than his partners; he wanted to fight, spill some blood, and his adrenaline rose just anticipating the next few minutes. That's the way he liked it. He wished that he could feel that way all the time.

Darrell walked up to his two minions with his weapon primed and wore a crooked smile as he said, "Time to play."

Don didn't hesitate any longer as he took the crowbar and shattered the backdoor lock of the restaurant. It splintered in seconds, the broken hardware fell to the ground, and then he kicked the door in. He dropped the crowbar to the side of the back entrance. There was barely any audible noise and the current late night employees were unaware of the intrusion.

The men entered and dispersed in three directions inside the restaurant.

Darrell didn't waste any time. He moved stealthily through the darkened kitchen until he could hear voices near the front entrance. Talking in regular conversation tones, the employees didn't have any idea that he was there or what was about to happen. He knew that they were counting the money from the day and that there would be at least twenty thousand dollars in cash just waiting for him. Most of the cash would be from the bar.

He slowed his pace when he saw the backs of the two employees' heads as they sat at the end of the bar. Two men in their early thirties were neatly stacking money and receipts from the day. There were two half-filled, foreign bottles of beer beside them. The rest of the restaurant and kitchen were dark and it was just the two men alone—just as he had expected.

A pot dropped onto the stainless counter in the kitchen, clanging noisily as it tumbled to the floor. Both men at the bar immediately turned in the direction of the noise and saw Darrell standing before them. They were shot before they could say a word. Darrell had fired two bullets, one in each chest. The men crumpled to the floor with gushing crimson quickly staining their starched, white shirts. Darrell began grabbing the cash and filling his pockets without a care in the world.

Don lumbered into the room with his shotgun locked and loaded. He managed a wry smile as he looked at the cold, hard cash on the bar. One of the employees began to move slightly on the floor and tried to crawl away in a last ditch effort to escape.

Three booming shotgun blasts obliterated the two employees' skulls. Bone and brain matter propelled by thick blood sprayed across the bar and floor. There was no identifiable faces left to resemble any person.

Don began to gather stacks of money and credit card receipts. He knew he could sell credit card numbers for some quick cash.

Ten feet away, Johnny stood mesmerized. He couldn't take his eyes away from the bodies and where their faces had been. The blood was still warm, dripping around the bar, and he wondered if they had felt anything or how long their brain actually continued functioning before it was technically dead. He didn't feel sad or anxious, just curious and calm. Don tossed him a stack of money, interrupting his thoughts.

All three men hurried to grab everything they could in the restaurant that might be worth something. It took about seven minutes and they were gone, leaving the carnage behind.

* * * * *

Inside the police cruiser Jack savored his third cup of strong, black coffee while parked near the Monterey wharf watching the evening lights sparkling on the bay. It had been a quiet night, which was fine by him. He was tired and wanted to get home. His shift was going to be over in about a half hour.

Jack reached between his seats and pulled out a medium-sized dog biscuit from a plain white bag. "Time for a Scooby snack?"

Keno barked happily from the back seat.

Jack flipped the doggie biscuit over his right shoulder and Keno caught it without hesitation, crunching it noisily from the backseat.

Occupying the passenger seat were several file folders, briefing notes, and three photographs of the most wanted criminals in Monterey and Santa Cruz counties. One of the photos showed a man by the name of Monty Stinger, a.k.a. Darrell Brooks, who was wanted for murder, kidnapping, and conspiracy to commit murder in several ongoing investigations at the sheriff's department.

Jack had his own thoughts about this case and the way he figured it, this man was going to kill again until the cops caught him. For some reason, this guy was able to boldly commit his crimes and then wreak havoc whenever he pleased, staying a couple steps ahead of the cops. That unnerved Jack and he wanted to learn everything he could about him and his previous crimes. He figured Darrell was connected to several murders that had been inconclusively connected to the act of a serial killer. His profile seemed to tick all the prerequisites of a serial killer and psychopathic personality.

The police radio crackled to life identifying his police code ID, interrupting his quiet break and investigative thoughts.

The female dispatcher said, "Mary twenty-four-thirty… copy?"

Jack responded into his car radio. "This is Mary twenty-four-thirty… go ahead."

"Jack… Tara called again."

Jack groaned and sighed. "I'm going to be home in an hour."

There was a slight pause and more radio activity before the dispatcher continued. "She said it was an emergency."

It's always an emergency.

He pressed the radio talk button. "Copy that."

Jack slowly took his cell phone out of his pocket and was just about to call Tara when a TRIPLE SOUND ALERT cut over the police radio.

Keno stood up in the back seat and let out a couple of high-pitched whines in eager anticipation.

The dispatcher instructed, "All available units, report of shots fired at 13216 Alvarado Street. Be advised of a late model gray van with two, possibly three, suspects leaving that location. Suspects are considered armed and extremely dangerous. Proceed with caution."

Jack quickly responded, "This is Mary twenty-four-thirty…I'm about three minutes from that location."

"Copy that."

Radio chatter erupted as more officers responded for assistance from other areas around the county at least ten to fifteen minutes away.

Jack dropped his patrol car into drive and didn't waste any time accelerating as fast as he could. The large engine hummed and revved as he left the parking lot, barely slowing over the speed bumps. Instantly, red and blue lights flashed to alert anyone that he was approaching. He kept the sirens off not to scare away the fleeing suspects. The night was completely deserted and he hadn't seen another car the entire time he was enjoying his coffee break.

CHAPTER FIVE

Jack was just about one minute from arriving at the restaurant and took a hard left turn, the tires making a familiar squeal in the process. His normally bright blue eyes turned to steel as he concentrated on catching those perps. He knew it was going to be dangerous, but he had hoped to catch them before they made it to a residential neighborhood where there could be more casualties and too many complications to worry about.

The quiet streets were suddenly interrupted by the gray van skidding onto the main street, barely missing the patrol car and then increasing speed once again. Dark cloudy smoke billowed from the loose tailpipe that kept the beat of the road, the engine pushed beyond the factory specifications.

Jack expertly recovered from the near collision, gaining his rightful position in the high-speed pursuit, cranking a one-eighty in the process. Keno barked three times as if to congratulate his partner on a masterful recovery, and was ready for action.

Jack reported into the radio, "I have the possible suspects in pursuit. Gray Dodge van…two, seven, Charlie, David, David, three. Now heading east on Del Monte Avenue."

Before Jack could put both hands back on the wheel, a black Mustang rocketed from a cross street and smashed the side of the police car.

The deafening crash was only two seconds of crumpled metal and glass as pieces of trim from both vehicles rained into the street and onto the sidewalk. The passenger side window of the patrol car had shattered and the crystallized pieces of the window dropped down in peculiar musical notes. Anything that wasn't secured in the front seat of the patrol car flew around in a haphazard display and finally landed on the floor and seat. The cool evening air instantly rushed into the car, cutting the heavy feeling of dread and the reality of what had just happened.

Jack could feel a slight pain shoot down to his lower back from the impact and a warm trickle of blood down his right cheek.

Keno was thrown to the floor, letting out a short yelp, and he began furiously working his four legs to maintain his upright balance, ready for anything at this point.

"Shit!" Jack exclaimed, recovering from the impact, absently wiping the blood from his cheek.

Jack glanced to the back seat to make sure his partner was okay before continuing pursuit. He saw Keno's large head poised at attention waiting for a command, intense black eyes staring straight ahead as he barked at the Mustang for taking off from the accident scene. Jack had no other choice but to pursue the suspect, keeping a constant visual on the fleeing vehicle.

Jack continued his report into the radio. "Second suspect in a black Mustang just hit me. License number is—"

He fought to maintain his place on the road and took a corner too short, tires squealing as the rear end slid from left to right.

Jack continued, "Three, eight, two, Adam, X-ray, four, Lincoln. Request back up units." He took a deep breath and pushed the patrol car to the limit, and prayed that no one was walking out late. "Suspects are turning right on David… proceeding southeast…"

Keno continued to bark incessantly—a deep, loud bark.

The van weaved back and forth across the median, trying desperately to shake its police pursuit. Pieces of the van's bumper, tailpipe, and a hubcap catapulted over two lanes, but it still managed to stay in the lead.

The Mustang kicked up its speed and passed the van expertly while missing the vehicle projectiles. It was no match for the police car, though, and the driver took every possible opportunity to gain an even bigger lead.

Jack wasn't giving up. He reported, "Proceeding south... approaching Highway 1."

Sirens and lights approached fast, filling the quiet streets. Two Monterey City police cars joined in the hot pursuit taking their positions behind Jack.

The Mustang easily glided through several intersections without regard to the red lights. It then made a bold right turn, hugging the road like an expert racecar driver crossing the finish line.

The van hit the same intersection, made the same right turn, but sideswiped a parked Volkswagen and a small pickup truck. It continued to fishtail, but somehow the tires managed to hang onto the pavement following the Mustang.

Jack couldn't believe both cars were still moving at the same accelerated speed. He continued, "Heading northbound on Highway 1."

Seaside Police and Monterey County sheriff cars joined the chase. Jack maintained his lead position and he wasn't going to lose the suspects. He could hear the patrol engine groan more than usual and wondered if the collision had damaged some of the vital working parts. He hoped that his vehicle wouldn't fail him now.

Only a couple of cars were driving on the freeway as the high-speed chase continued northbound away from the Monterey Bay. Speeds increased to over one hundred miles per hour, sometimes 120, and then back to ninety-five.

The two fleeing vehicles took an off ramp from the highway into the Fort Ord area on the outskirts of the city. It was a mostly abandoned military base with only a few occupied buildings. Many of the residential houses were vacant and dark, and there were rows of streets that resembled a modern day ghost town along the coastline.

The road quickly turned to dirt and gravel in desperate need of repaving. Heavy clouds of dust marred the vision of the pursuing police cars causing them to slow their pace.

* * * * *

The Mustang took advantage of the road conditions and pulled ahead and then down a dark street, cutting the headlights. It finally slowed and parked next to a dilapidated military building that once housed an officer's quarters. Darrell's bold move paid off as he sat and watched the police pursuit of the van. He could hear more police cars coming so he waited until it was all clear.

It was perfect timing. Darrell disappeared as quickly as he had arrived on the scene. He was going to get rid of the smashed Mustang and find himself another car before the cops were wise to him. He slowly drove away, turning on his headlights when he was a safe distance. He knew that Don and Johnny would most likely be caught, but they would never give him up—never.

* * * * *

40

Several rundown warehouses sat unattended with a chain link fence around them. They'd once housed army supplies and surplus from another time and had served their purpose, but now looked like only the paranormal would be residing in them.

The van barreled up the short driveway to the gated entrance, accelerated and crashed through the gate. It slammed open and the rusted hinges easily snapped under the extreme pressure. Smoke poured out from under the van's hood and the engine started knocking.

Jack was close behind and drove through the broken gate. He said into the police radio, "Suspects in van entered the old Fort Ord surplus warehouses on Admiral Way…lost visual on black Mustang."

Intense bright lights illuminated the industrial yard as a helicopter circled above and added more cover for the police. It swooped once around the area and zeroed in on the van with the brightest spotlight.

All the following police cars entered through the gate and skillfully took their positions in formation expecting immediate gunfire—or worse. Several more police cars entered the warehouse yard, including more K9 units, and took their cover positions.

The van finally slowed next to a four-story military warehouse; the front passenger doors flung wide open and both men immediately leaped out, running before the van had completely stopped. The van suddenly lurched forward and crashed into a retaining wall, crumpling the front bumper.

Don and Johnny sprinted off in different directions around the building and into the shadowy warehouse. The van's radiator busted wide open as hot steam spewed out into the night. The floating mist continued to seep into the darkness with a ghostly haze.

CHAPTER SIX

Jack cautiously emerged with his gun drawn from his patrol car, leaving Keno to wait, agitated and wanting to get to work. The other officers followed Jack's example and guardedly took cover behind their vehicles. All cops were ready for a gun battle, if necessary, and they weren't going to let those men get away no matter the circumstances.

Two Seaside police officers carefully approached the barely idling van, keeping their bodies low and the vehicle as cover. They both checked the interior before cutting the ignition. The taller officer gave the "all clear" signal to the rest of the anxiously waiting group.

Four Sheriff's deputies stealthily made their way around the perimeter of the warehouse and took cover. They waited for further instructions or until all hell broke loose.

Jack announced in the radio loudspeaker, "This is the Monterey County Sheriff's Office, surrender and come out with your hands up! Come out with your hands up now!"

Everyone waited and watched intently.

No response.

A few of the officers were twitchy and edgy, not knowing what to expect next. Eyes were trained on any possible exit of the warehouse or the glimpse of a protruding firearm. A wide range of law enforcement experience now focused on the two perps inside the building. Some police officers were merely rookies with only a couple years on the force, while others were seasoned and had taken down their fair share of bad guys over the years.

The warehouse remained strangely quiet and dark, except for the lights of the emergency vehicles dancing around the open areas. Other than a few canine barks, it was quiet. Guns from all directions were pointed at any possible exit. No one spoke; even the police radio was silent.

Nothing.

A tall, older sheriff's sergeant approached Jack from his own K9 cruiser with a large German shepherd in the back. His short, salt and pepper hair made him appear to be the wise one of the group. Even though he was in his late fifties, he was experienced and in top physical condition that kept him keenly alert and capable. His eyes told another story; they were kind but dark from things he had witnessed in his thirty-two year career of keeping the streets in order and civilians safe.

Jack moved to the trunk area of his cruiser to meet up with his sergeant. Sergeant Alec Weaver had been his mentor and friend for as long as he'd been with the department. He was the training officer for all of the K9 units.

Weaver explained the situation. "They shot a restaurant owner and bartender at the end of 16th. It was brutal and they have nothing to lose now. I'll take in Sam with two cover officers, Rominger and Sullivan."

Jack glanced over to see the two cover officers getting ready to enter the building. Disappointed, he looked hard at his sergeant, but didn't say a word.

A tall, blond sheriff's K9 deputy in his early thirties approached Jack. "Send in Keno or should I get Booker?" he asked.

All police dogs began barking incessantly.

Jack took a deep breath and answered Deputy McPherson, "You and Romero cover me and Keno."

Weaver looked at Jack. "Keno ready?"

"More than ready." Jack looked up at the warehouse. "We'll take the third and fourth floors."

"Fine. I'll take the first and second," Weaver said as he looked at his cover team. "Let's go."

The sergeant pushed a remote control on his utility belt to open the back car door of his cruiser and Sam jumped out. Obediently, the large shepherd padded to him and the sergeant snapped on his lead.

A smug looking, stocky, dark-haired officer made a point to brush past Jack, shouldered him slightly, and gave a phony smile. "Be careful up there," he said.

Jack stopped abruptly and turned to face the officer who was already following Sergeant Weaver.

McPherson stepped up next to his friend. "Forget about Rominger. He's an asshole who hasn't figured that out yet."

Jack smiled and knew he was right, but he still couldn't shake the feeling that he was being undermined every time he turned around, and he hated that fact.

"C'mon, let's go," McPherson said as Romero joined him and they both waited for Jack.

Jack opened the back door to his patrol car and Keno jumped out. In his excitement and frustration at not being able to catch a bad guy yet, the dog took several circular spins. Jack clipped a long leather lead on the Labrador and led his group to the warehouse to gain access up to the third floor. Keno jogged in perfect sync with his human partner as his shiny black coat glistened in between the emergency lights of the patrol cars and police officers.

* * * * *

The main entrance of the warehouse showed that two of the rusted locks had been broken in three pieces, likely recently. It was obvious the two fleeing suspects had easily broken the locks and it was to their fortune for the moment, but their luck was soon going to change.

Sergeant Weaver and Sam took their positions just to the right side of the entrance and allowed for deputies Rominger and Sullivan to clear the entrance first.

Weaver yelled, "Sheriff's Office! Come out with your hands up or we will send in the dog!" He paused. There was nothing from inside. "Sheriff's Office! Come out or we'll send in the dog!"

The team waited, barely breathing. Silence continued, except for Sam's whines and barks. The sergeant could barely hold the leash.

Rominger kicked open the door.

They entered the first floor and fanned out.

* * * * *

Jack and his cover officers managed to climb the rickety back staircase to the third floor. The stairs creaked and groaned under their weight, but it didn't slow down their pursuit. McPherson and Romero kept a watchful eye on the windows they passed.

All three police officers used their flashlights to see what could possibly be lurking in the darkness waiting to ambush them.

Keno kept his nose down and picked up a scent. His muscular neck seemed to expand as he climbed the stairs effortlessly. He didn't need any extra illumination to see and his dark coat rendered him a chameleon in the darkness.

The group reached the top and Jack broke a small window to a side door. Deputies McPherson and Romero checked the entrance from left to right before they entered.

* * * * *

Inside the first floor of the warehouse, Sergeant Weaver and his team took appropriate cover and cleared the area. In the beams of flashlights, they saw overturned metal furniture: desks, bookshelves, single beds, and broken up tables and chairs. Toward the back of the area were several closed cabinets. Everything was covered in thick cobwebs and heavy dust. It looked more like the makings of a large bonfire than supplies for a military base.

Weaver unhooked Sam's leash and gave the command, "Sam, search!"

Sam didn't waste a single moment and padded around the room, picking up a scent and then dismissing it. He kept his nose high to get a radar on the suspects.

All officers visually swept the first floor quickly and it found it empty.

Deputy Rominger yelled, "Clear!"

Followed by Sullivan's booming voice, "Clear!"

Sam continued to move around the old rusty pieces of equipment and furniture, weaving in and out systematically until he approached the stairs leading up to the next floor.

Weaver followed and read his dog in the process. "Sam, down!"

Obediently, the dog sat down at the bottom of the staircase but clearly wanted to continue. He watched his partner and eagerly waited for his next command.

Weaver gave the first update on the radio, "First floor clear."

* * * * *

Keno stood at a tall metal cabinet on the third floor barking viciously while his every developed muscle twitched. His white teeth almost glowed in the shadowy warehouse.

The doors on the cabinet were closed so it was impossible to tell if there was anyone hiding inside.

The tension rose exponentially in the room.

Jack had his flashlight beam and gun trained on the cabinet, ready for anything to come bursting out. "Sheriff's office! Come out now!" he ordered.

Romero covered McPherson as he slid up next to the large cabinet. He looked at his fellow officers and wordlessly conveyed what he was going to do.

They all nodded in agreement.

McPherson grabbed the rusty handle, slowly turned the grip down, and then flung the cabinet door wide open with a crash.

Keno leaped forward before Jack could respond. His fear was that the dog was jumping into a dangerous—possibly fatal—situation.

All officers rushed up to the cabinet, but only a couple of unlabeled canisters fell out, thumping on the floor and rolling precariously to the corner.

Keno's large paws raked over a crowbar that was the only thing in the cabinet that was potentially dangerous. He worked both paws and it was obvious to the officers that Keno had discovered a fresh scent on it.

Jack exclaimed, "Shit!"

"Looks like they thought this might not be a good place to hide," McPherson stated.

"Keno, search!" Jack ordered.

Keno hesitated at the location and then continued his search around the room. The officers scanned and quickly searched the area but found no suspects.

Jack reported into the police radio, "Third floor clear."

* * * * *

Sergeant Weaver and his two cover officers searched the second floor diligently, directing their flashlights around the large room behind cabinets and into the tight corners. The beams of light generated even more shadows and eerie distortions around the room.

There was nothing except littered garbage and large unrecognizable items that should have been taken to the dump years ago. The smell of mold and old trash permeated all of the cops' senses, making them unconsciously wrinkle their noses with disgust as they continued their search.

It didn't, however, divert Sam from his important duty of finding the bad guys. He alternated his keen canine nose from high to low trying to keep the fresh human scent alive. He moved toward one of the corners and began to gain speed to step around old food processing equipment.

Johnny jumped up like a Jack-in-the-Box and aimed his gun at the officers, but it took not two seconds before Sam locked his jaws onto the perp's shoulder. Both criminal and dog went down hard on the floor in a mass of fur, arms, and legs. The Glock 19 handgun clattered across the floor and almost rested perfectly against Sergeant Weaver's combat boots.

Johnny's shrill scream was startling enough without the growling dog attached to him.

"Lay down! Don't move!" Sergeant Weaver said as he approached the whimpering suspect.

Deputy Rominger kicked the gun farther away from the suspect and pushed his shotgun toward the fighting man. "Stay down! Don't fight!"

"Get it off me! Get it off me!" was the only thing Johnny could say between breaths and screams.

"Quit fighting!" the deputies yelled.

Johnny finally realized his situation was futile and quit moving, but covered his head in a feeble attempt to stay safe. He looked like a small, weak child trying to get the attention of his mother.

"Sam, off! Come!" Weaver ordered.

Instantly, Sam let go of Johnny and trotted over next to the sergeant, wagging his tail the entire time. His lead was quickly snapped back on.

"Good boy," Weaver said and smiled as he patted the dog. "Good boy, Sam."

Deputy Sullivan had his handcuffs out. "Lay flat! Put your arms out now!"

Johnny quickly put his arms out and the deputy clicked on the handcuffs and did a quick frisk. Rominger covered, while the other deputy pulled the whining man to his feet.

"That dog's crazy, man! It bit the shit out of me."

Deputy Rominger smiled and said, "We warned ya."

"It bit me!" he insisted.

Weaver got directly in Johnny's face. "Where's your buddy?"

"Fuck you and your dog!"

Weaver spoke into the police radio. "One suspect in custody. We're coming out."

All three officers and Sam with their prisoner emerged from the warehouse's main entrance. With some relief, the two deputies put Johnny in the back of a patrol car and slammed the door.

The tension remained high as the backup officers watched the sergeant and dog approach. The K9 team walked across the parking area; Sam with his big, beautiful head with ears alert appeared to be strutting in front of the rest of the officers.

All assisting cops looked up to the top two floors of the warehouse from their safe locations. They could see light flashing back and forth from the fourth floor through some of the broken windows, casting an abnormal freakish lightshow through the broken glass. If they strained, they could hear voices yelling back and forth. All they could do was wait and hope that their brothers in blue would safely exit the building with the second suspect.

CHAPTER SEVEN

With Keno, Jack diligently searched the cluttered and partially dilapidated top floor. As the flashlights beamed throughout the area, it was obvious to Jack that the second suspect was close—he could feel it deep within his core.

Keno was focused on his job, but he kept coming back to some old bags of potting soil in the middle of the floor.

Jack, annoyed by Keno's distraction, commanded, "Keno, search!"

The dog padded once around the room, completely disinterested, and came back to the bags of soil. This time he scratched furiously at them and barked twice.

Jack, along with his cover officers McPherson and Romero, took one last look around the room for any potential hiding place.

Nothing.

The three officers looked at one another questioningly.

McPherson offered an explanation. "Maybe he thinks it's a place to take a crap?"

Jack ignored him. "Something's up." He commanded more forcefully, "Keno, search!"

"This guy couldn't have gotten out without anyone seeing him." McPherson spoke softly, actually talking to himself rather than the group.

Deputy Romero shined his flashlight inspecting the bags, and moved one fifty-pound bag carefully to the side. The ripped bags revealed several fresh, dirty footprints on a few of them. He exclaimed, "Here. Check it out."

The beam of light uncovered what had attracted Keno's attention. The deputy raised the light toward the ceiling and saw a broken skylight.

Jack praised Keno. "Good boy." He then reported into the radio to the command center outside, "Fourth floor is clear. Suspect is hiding on the roof. We're going up."

The officers moved some of the bags closer to the wooden ladder leading to the roof. With some difficulty, Jack and Keno went first to the skylight opening.

"Right behind you, partner," said McPherson, shining his flashlight in front of them.

Keno was the first to reach the opening. Jack easily popped the escape hatch and hoisted the dog onto the roof. Instantly, Keno took off barking into the darkness.

The three deputies scrambled their way onto the roof, careful to keep their peripherals of any potential danger in the shadows. The two cover officers took cover as Jack moved toward Keno.

A piercing scream filled the night.

Keno appeared from the darkened side of the roof dragging the flailing suspect by his thigh toward the waiting police. Don continued to scream in horror as the muscular dog kept a strong bite hold on him.

"Keno, off!" Jack yelled.

The three deputies took positions with their weapons pointed at the suspect. As soon as Keno let go of Don's leg, he managed to scramble back toward the edge of the rooftop.

All three officers yelled commands at the same time for the man to comply.

Keno kept barking and approaching the desperate suspect.

"Stop! I said stop!"

"Get down on the ground now!"

"Show me some hands! Get down now!"

"Stop!"

"Keno, bite!"

Without missing a step, Keno jumped on Don again, sunk his teeth deep into his shoulder and effortlessly took him down to the rooftop. Don fought with all his strength, but he wasn't a match for the trained, strong canine. Keno adjusted his bites several times, inflicting several new bites on Don's shoulder to keep hold of him.

Don stopped moving. He was still as his face looked out over the edge of the roof.

"Keno, off!" commanded Jack.

The dog obediently padded over to Jack for his praise.

With caution, the cover officers moved in closer to Don.

McPherson said, "Don't move! Let's see some hands now!" He inched closer to the suspect.

The officers on the ground watched the scene unfold on the rooftop, waiting helplessly for what was going to happen next.

McPherson pushed the shotgun closer to the suspect while his partner holstered his weapon. Romero was just about to put the handcuffs on Don who leaped up in an out-of-control frenzy and knocked the officers back.

McPherson quickly regained his balance and scrambled toward Don. "Get down on the ground now!"

Keno bolted forward, running at top speed, dove between McPherson's legs, and jumped on Don once again.

In only a split second, everything and everyone had changed positions.

Following the hard impact, Don and Keno fought on the edge of the rooftop. Don lost his balance and began to slide over the edge of the decaying roof, slowly taking Keno with him.

Jack yelled out in horror, "Keno, come!"

Keno tried to retreat backwards from his attack, but Don grabbed hold of the dog's collar and began to pull both of them over the edge to a drop of more than four stories below.

Jack lunged forward and dove onto his belly to assist his partner. He took hold of the dog's back legs and then began to work his way to the chest, and then to the collar. Jack hooked his arm around Keno's chest and with the other hand, gripped his collar.

Quickly, McPherson and Romero joined Jack and formed a human chain to hold onto the K9 unit.

Don tried to get his footing on the old crumbling roof, dangling precariously with his overweight body. Each attempt he made only helped to pull Keno closer to the edge—which would be to their deaths.

The trailing officers slowly began to lose their footing.

Breathlessly, Jack pleaded, "Keno, come! C'mon, boy!" To the other officers, he ordered, "Don't let go!" He then reached for Don. "Let go of the dog and take my hand."

McPherson grimaced as his muscles burned. "Don't know how much longer I can hold on!"

Keno remained low, stretching his muscular neck. His paws scraped along the rooftop.

Don didn't care anymore and wasn't going to be arrested under any condition. "Fuck you!" he seethed.

Jack insisted, "Grab my hand! You're going to fall! Take my hand and let go of the collar!"

Don stopped struggling and stared directly at Jack for an intense moment. He smiled and said, "If I go, the dog's going with me." With both hands gripping tightly on the collar, he let his full hefty weight pull down on Keno and the officers.

"NO!" Jack wasn't going to let Keno die this way. "PULL!"

Keno let out a ferocious bark as he squirmed his way out of the collar, which easily slipped off the dog's head as Don disappeared over the edge and into the night.

Silence.

Stunned, all three officers rolled onto their backs to catch their breath. Jack scrambled to Keno to check for any visible injuries. The officers could hear voices and shouts from below and they slowly got up and looked down.

Don was lying face down in a river of his own blood as officers rushed to him with their guns drawn. Even in death, his right hand clutched Keno's police collar that accompanied a shiny badge.

Only a few feet away, from the back of the police car, Johnny watched his dead partner in crime bleed out. He kicked the inside of the police car furiously, cussing the police.

Emergency vehicles made their way to the scene as the helicopter flashed the spotlight one more time before it turned and headed off to assist in another pursuit.

CHAPTER EIGHT

It was early in the morning and the sun was just beginning to rise over the hills, casting a beautiful reddish-orange glow. The roads were still deserted even for the earliest commuters. A few birds bustled in the sparse trees across the paved parking lot. Three cars slowly drove in and found parking places.

The diverse Monterey County in California had more than 400,000 residents. At any given time, the Monterey County jail housed more than twelve hundred inmates in the stark, cement building complete with barbed wire and electrified fences. It was a detention facility for men and women who were awaiting trial or transportation to one of the many prisons in the state of California.

Just northeast of the jail was the Monterey County Sheriff's Administration building that housed the deputies, forensic lab, the sheriff himself, and was open to the public during regular business hours. It was a working building that ran twenty-four hours a day along with the jail.

A secure outside door from the administrative building opened, as Jack—along with his faithful four-legged partner—exited, heading to his truck. He was finally finished with the necessary paperwork of the long night. Exhausted, all he wanted to do was go home and get some sleep.

A group of young officers just coming on duty for the day shift passed Jack and Keno, but not without expressing their many congratulations with high-fives, including plenty of fun '*kudos*' and '*atta boys*' for Keno.

The dog seemed to raise his large head higher with every compliment he received.

Deputy McPherson joined Jack in the parking lot. He made a point to pat Keno on the back. "Awesome job, partner."

"You too," Jack said and smiled.

"I was talking to Keno."

"Funny."

"What would we do without our partners?" McPherson stopped at his black truck where his four-legged partner waited, jumping from seat to seat, ready to go.

"I never want to find out," said Jack. "See you in a couple of days."

"See ya."

Jack opened the passenger door to his two-tone brown truck and Keno easily jumped inside. He then tossed his duffle bag on the floor and shut the door. Within a few seconds, he was on his way home.

Finally.

It took Jack almost a half hour to get home to Pacific Grove. Traffic was light and he made great time. He took 6th Street off Lighthouse and pulled into a small cobblestone driveway. A small, one story, stucco house—complete with colorful flowers in small window boxes—led to the charm of the neighborhood and small coastal town. Most houses were small and the properties were extremely close together, but his neighbors were nice and appreciated a police officer living in the neighborhood.

Jack cut the engine.

Keno was excited to be home, too, and jumped over Jack to the outdoors to pay a visit to a familiar bush.

Jack grabbed his duffle bag, shut his door, and secured the alarm. He smiled to himself because nothing ever happened in his neighborhood, but it was a habit to press the alarm button. Sleep was the only thing on his mind and he hoped that Tara wasn't in one of her moods like so many other mornings.

"C'mon, Keno," he said.

The black dog caught up with Jack and joined him at the front door with his thick tail wagging with delight. Two empty boxes sat to the left side of the door. Jack thought this strange, but weary as he was, he didn't care.

Jack used his key and opened the front door. Keno zoomed by him and ran around the living room, continuing to run until he was at the back sliding door where a happy Golden Retriever waited. Both dogs chased each other on opposite sides of the glass with their familiar game of doggie tag.

In shock, Jack stood at the threshold of his house—empty except for an old black recliner chair, dining table and chairs, and a few items on the bookshelves, including Jack's baseball collection and throwing knives. It looked like the house had been robbed or had been prepared to be shown to potential buyers. All pictures and personal items had been taken off the walls. The large sofa, chairs, and coffee table were gone. The only thing that remained to remind Jack that the furniture had once been there were the clean spots on the tan carpet.

"What the—?"

He tossed his duffle bag and jacket on the floor next to a partially crumpled photo of himself and a pretty blonde woman. He saw an envelope addressed to him on the kitchen counter and picked it up. He knew what it would say and why, but he was going to read it anyway.

Jack,

We've drifted apart for too long now and we will never find our way back. I've moved on and I'm happy for once in a very long time with Blake. I hope that you will find what makes you happy.

–Tara

He leaned against the counter for support. Even though he knew what the note would say, it didn't change the fact that it stung. He and Tara had been together for five years and there'd been some good times, but lately she'd been indifferent to him and unhappy with what he could give her. He'd known the relationship was ultimately going to end. It was for the best.

Keno had moved next to Jack and rubbed his head against his hand as if to let him know in his canine way that everything was going to be okay.

"Well, it's just you, me, and Tina now." He looked at the patient dog waiting at the sliding door wagging her tail furiously.

Jack opened the sliding door and both dogs began running around the open house, happy to see each other.

It was almost as if Jack had been in a bad dream and he just couldn't wake up yet. He needed to get a glass of water and catch his breath. He opened a cupboard to find it completely empty except for one plastic glass and one plastic plate. In frustration, he took the glass and threw it across the room. That was all he could do under the circumstances.

Curiously, Keno went to investigate the cup on the floor and limped on his front legs in the process.

CHAPTER NINE

A large estate resided on a hill overlooking the view of the beautiful Monterey Bay. There were many windows from which the occupants could enjoy the breathtaking views. There was never a bad view to be seen. The yards were simple with artistic rocks and paths that meandered along with carefully placed trees and flowers. Meticulously groomed and upscale, there wasn't anything out of place at the Carmel residence.

A white minivan pulled into the half-circle driveway and stopped just a few feet from the stairs leading to the main entrance. A plump woman in her early fifties got out and proceeded to slide open the back car door, finding a dozen bags of groceries neatly tucked in together. She grabbed two of the bags and made her way to the front door, huffing in the process.

The entryway opened into a large foyer, and then into a spacious living room. The large greeting room spread out to incorporate the kitchen, study, and family room. To one side of the family room were several antique desks arranged in a functional, work-oriented manner with computers and phones. The neat desktops were organized with clever accessory holders.

A young, barefoot woman with shoulder-length blonde hair and dressed in blue jeans and a loose t-shirt entered the room carrying a box of paperwork and a couple of steno notepads. A large yellow Labrador Retriever followed closely behind her and finally took his usual sleeping spot on a doggie bed next to one of the desks.

Just as she pulled some paperwork out of the box, the front door opened and she heard a breathless, enthusiastic voice. "Hello, hello! Oh, hi, Megan. How are you today?"

Megan put down her paperwork. "I'm fine, Diane. How many more bags do you have?"

Not missing a beat, Diane said, "I think that I've got you and your sister stocked up for a while."

"That's great," Megan said and followed Diane to the kitchen. "Thank you. I was going to try and go, but it wasn't a good morning for me. I'm working on it." She hesitated for a moment and continued. "I really am."

"It's okay, Megan. If you're not ready, you're just not ready." With motherly concern, she patted Megan's hand.

Megan hated feeling like she was a prisoner of her own doing. She knew that she just needed more confidence to get out and live her life. Sometimes her medications were helping and other times they made things worse. She took a deep breath and told herself that it was all going to work out.

Her striking sister, Teresa, entered the kitchen, interrupting Megan's thoughts. She was a tall, slender woman with dark hair dressed in a sharp business suit. There was a definite family resemblance, but Teresa was taller with more angular features. She helped herself to a cup of coffee.

Megan said, "I didn't hear you come in last night."

"I thought that I was the older sister?" she joked.

"Everything okay?"

Teresa smiled thinly. "Of course." She quickly changed the subject. "Why did you cancel your session with Dr. Marshall this morning?"

Megan tried to ignore the question by helping unload groceries as Diane made several trips from the car to the kitchen.

"Is there a problem?" Teresa persisted.

"I'm feeling better," Megan muttered.

"I don't think you should—"

Megan interrupted. "I'm fine, Teresa. I'm feeling much better and I've got a lot of work to do anyway."

"I just want you to feel better and enjoy life again, outside of this house."

Megan softened a bit. "I know…I will. I promise."

Teresa looked at her watch and put her coffee cup down. "Gotta go. Be back later."

"Where are you going?" Megan asked, watching her sister with some curiosity.

"If you need me, just call my cell phone." Teresa didn't wait for her younger sister to interrogate her every movement. She quickly left and shut the front door softly behind her.

Megan continued to put away groceries as she wondered where her sister was going. She didn't bother to tell Teresa that she knew she wasn't going to work anymore. Wherever Teresa was going, it must have been important. Teresa had been somewhat distant after the death of her husband and had never quite recovered from the shock. Megan gave her sister space whenever she needed it. That was how they could get along and share the house.

Megan obsessed over where Teresa was and why it was such a secret. So many scenarios ran through her mind and all the possible scenarios she imagined seemed to be getting worse. She couldn't stop herself from her mild mania when it was something that she didn't have control over.

CHAPTER TEN

On the west side of Castroville there sat a small motel with fourteen rooms. Set back a little bit from the main road, most motorists and residents wouldn't notice the rundown place, or perhaps didn't want to admit that it was even there.

A weather-beaten sign read *Cozy Inn by the Bay*.

It was the type of motel that attracted occupants who didn't want to be found or who had something to hide from the rest of the world—usually the criminal element. Two of the most popular activities here—daytime or nighttime—were drug dealing or prostitution.

Three cars were parked out in front of the single level motel. One of the three cars didn't have two back tires, but the other two hadn't moved since the day before. Every motel door was painted a different southwestern color. At one time, it might have been pleasing to the eye, but now it screamed poverty, crime, and the need for some serious maintenance. The flowerbeds were empty, now containing only the trampled trash of nearby fast food restaurants from the overnight guests. The water of the small kidney-shaped pool was brown with a thick layer of leaves from nearby trees and it only attracted mosquitoes. It had been years since anyone had actually gone swimming.

It was the rest stop for Darrell who was tucked inside room #7. He liked that he had a lucky number room in which to rest for the night. He had dumped the souped-up Mustang in Marina and had opted for an older Honda with license plates from another abandoned car. It was perfect because this car blended into the community and no one would notice him.

It took him a while to unwind after the killings and high-speed chase. He had really wanted to take the police on a wild goose chase and taunt them some more; they needed to know who was calling all the shots. They were stupid and it was becoming obvious to Darrell that they were never going to catch him. He could do whatever he pleased and take anything he wanted—at any time he wanted.

Darrell was still partially dressed in his black jeans and dark t-shirt as he slept peacefully. The drapes were drawn tight. The scummy bedspread was wadded and tossed on the floor in the corner. He slept on top of the sheets with two pillows. The nightstand held his Glock with two extra clips along with several empty beer bottles and a cell phone. An ashtray on the small table in the middle of the room was filled with dozens of smoked cigarettes and two hamburger supreme wrappers.

There were remnants of heroin paraphernalia that had helped him to relax and keep everything in focus. A bottle of a high potent sleep aid was toppled on its side with only four pills left. He used whatever he could from time to time so that he could get some sleep. It seemed that the devil wasn't far away at any given time, and drug and alcohol induced sleep was the only way to keep the dark one away.

The cell phone rang.

Darrell groaned and stirred slightly, but he didn't make a move to answer it.

It stopped.

A few minutes later, it rang again.

He clumsily reached his hand toward the nightstand and knocked the phone onto the floor. As it landed precariously, the speaker phone button had been activated.

After a brief silence, Darrell could hear the sound of someone breathing. A crisp, authoritative voice said, "Pick up the phone, Darrell."

Recognizing the voice immediately, he swung his legs over the side of the bed, bent down, and picked up the cell phone. He pushed the talk button to take it off speaker.

"Hello?" His voice was scratchy and his throat felt like he hadn't had a drink in a month. The room seemed to shift and his head felt like it was underwater. He hated being summoned while he was enjoying a restful sleep. He held his tongue and pressed the phone tighter against his ear to channel some of the intense energy he felt.

He listened for two minutes as he was told about the events of the previous evening. "Yeah," he murmured. He was becoming more awake and could feel his anger building in disbelief at what he was hearing.

"The cops killed him?" He listened to more about Johnny. "What about bail?" He listened to more explanations. "Can you get him out?" The answer was yes and then the phone went dead.

Darrell lit another cigarette and slowly inhaled. "Fucking cops," he said as he exhaled.

There was a knock at the door.

Instinctively, Darrell grabbed his Glock and released the safety. He quickly moved toward the entrance, unlocked the flimsy security chain, and cracked open the door. He put the safety back on and tucked the gun into his waistband. He opened the door wider and Teresa entered still dressed in her business suit.

"Hi, baby, I missed you." She slipped her arms around his waist.

"I wasn't expecting you until later," he said.

"You know I have to keep up with the appearance of going to work."

Darrell kissed her roughly and pressed her up against the wall. "You're here with me now."

CHAPTER ELEVEN

Megan had been working nonstop on the computer after Diane and Teresa had left. She felt more alert and confident when she was working, and didn't dwell on her current condition. It was called a condition, or rather a mental disorder, and she hated that fact more than anything. She had been diagnosed with agoraphobia a few years before, but it wasn't at the full-blown stage and sometimes she was able to handle activities outside the comfort of her own home. Other times, she suffered and felt that she needed the relief and safety of her house.

Megan had two computers working as she designed websites and blogs for two of her clients. One was a sporting goods store and the other was an insurance company. The one thing for which she was thankful was that she could work at home on her own terms. She didn't actually need to work because her grandparents had left her and Teresa more than they could ever spend in a lifetime, but working was better therapy than any drug or shopping spree.

Her dog, Eddie, was sleeping in his designated area where he could be close to Megan and still know what was going on in the household.

Without warning, Eddie cried out in pain.

"Eddie?" Megan stopped typing and looked down at her dog.

The dog had turned on his side, softly whining, and soon his breathing became shallow and rapid. Megan dropped to her knees to try and comfort her dog. She ran her hand near his stomach and he cried out in pain.

"I've got to get you to the vet."

She ran to the phone and dialed, then waited.

Teresa's cell phone was on the passenger seat in her car in front of the motel. It rang without anyone hearing it.

"C'mon, Teresa, please pick up." Megan felt her chest tighten and her breathing quickened. "Please pick up... *please*..." She couldn't stop herself from crying.

She threw down her receiver and it crashed on the living room floor. She quickly went back to Eddie and he seemed to be getting worse by the second. She tried to catch her breath, but her fear and anxiety were taking over her body. The more she fought it, the more it took over.

She jumped up and ran to the kitchen, and snatched a set of car keys hanging on a peg. Seconds later, she was at the front door and she flung it open wide. That was as far as she got. She stood at the threshold, still inside the house.

Her view of the front yard distorted. The sides of the house looked askew and the stairs moved as if they were floating on the water. Everything came in and out of focus leaving her with a chronic feeling of vertigo.

Megan was paralyzed with fear.

It was a fear of the unknown of what could happen if she left the house. Her conscious, rational mind knew that nothing out of the ordinary was going to happen and that she was going to be just fine. It was her irrational fear and strange feelings of fight or flight that took hold of her.

It didn't matter now. Megan didn't care about herself. She was going to get Eddie to the vet no matter what. She should have run out down the stairs to the car in the driveway, but instead, she took two steps onto the porch and froze. She cursed aloud; she wanted to run but her body stopped her. She gripped the side of the front door and her sweaty hands couldn't get a hold on the house without slipping off.

She felt herself falling as her field of vision narrowed.

Pulling herself into a tight fetal position only two feet from the front door, she gasped, "I can do this." She fought hard to keep from throwing up.

"I can do this," she repeated.

She moved toward the stairs and she focused on one at a time. Stumbling a couple of times, she managed to make it to the car at the end of the driveway.

It took a few tries, but she managed to push the unlock button on the key chain. Her shaking, sweaty hand opened the driver's car door and she plopped down in the comfortable leather seat. The ignition caught and she jammed the car into reverse, backing up as far as the entrance stairs.

She now was running on sheer terror and adrenaline as she made her way into the house and returned with Eddie in her arms. She wasn't quite sure where she found the strength to carry a seventy-five pound dog, but she did. His lifeless legs bounced as she got to the car, then she put him on the backseat.

Megan didn't remember driving to the vet's office or even her feelings of fear. She didn't care because now anger had taken over and she wanted to help her faithful companion.

* * * * *

Keno sat up straight on the examination table, and that would ensure he got even more attention. He was a little uncomfortable, but he loved Dr. Reynolds and his assistant, Marisa.

Jack and Dr. Reynolds examined Keno's front legs. The vet massaged and worked his joints and foot. Keno couldn't help but give the vet a quick lick to the side of his face.

Dr. Reynolds explained, "The x-rays looked fine. Maybe just a little overextended."

"We had a big scuffle last night." Jack still couldn't get the vision out of his mind of Keno being pulled off of the roof.

The vet continued, "He should be fine with a little bit of rest. Keep an eye on him and definitely bring him back if he doesn't get any better."

The young veterinary assistant entered the examination room with tons of bubbly energy as she gave the doctor a syringe. "Here you go, Dr. Reynolds." She smiled at Jack and looked to Keno. "Keno, you're a big, beautiful police dog." She lovingly petted his head and scratched behind his ears. "I didn't know Labs were patrol dogs, I thought they were just sniffer dogs."

Jack smiled because he had heard this comment so many times. "Keno's one of the exceptions."

The doctor expertly gave Keno an injection. "This is an anti-inflammatory that will help with any swelling and make him feel better."

Just then, there was the sound of frantic knocking on the back door emergency entrance. Marisa went to the door and quickly returned with a grim expression. "It's Megan. Eddie's sick."

Jack looked to the back entrance and saw a barefoot woman carrying a large yellow Labrador that wasn't moving. Quickly, Dr. Reynolds helped her carry the dog to the second examination room.

The woman was breathing hard and walking stilted, like she was going to fall over any moment. Marisa came to her assistance and helped her to a chair and gave her a glass of water. Marisa was patient and kind. "It's okay, Megan...breathe easy. Everything is going to be fine. Drink some water and try to relax. Breathe."

The woman tried to drink the water, but seemed to find it difficult.

Jack approached her. "Megan?" He was surprised to see her, but he hardly recognized her.

She slowly looked up at Jack. "Jack...oh, Jack..."

Megan stood up and threw her weak arms around him. They embraced for a couple of moments.

Jack tried to soothe her. "It's okay."

"You two know each other?" Marisa looked surprised.

Megan weakly whispered into Jack's ear. "I'm so glad that you're here."

"We've known each other since we were kids and then reconnected online a few months ago," Jack explained, still holding Megan. "We haven't seen each other in four or five years."

Dr. Reynolds returned with a solemn look on his face. "I'm sorry, Megan. There was nothing I could do."

"No," she sobbed.

"All signs indicated that he had been poisoned."

Megan began to cry harder on Jack's shoulders. He held her tight, feeling sick as he constantly feared for Keno's safety from people who would mean to hurt him since he was a police dog.

CHAPTER TWELVE

The large conference room was filled with some of the most highly educated and driven attorneys in the state of California. A more accurate description would be that the room was filled with some of the most ruthless defense attorneys ever born. You would better hope that you weren't being sued by Winston, Palmer, Chamberlain, Hayward & Associates.

The two partners and seven associates at the huge mahogany table were comfortably seated in plush, overstuffed leather chairs. For as comfortable as the chairs were, most of the associates were completely miserable. It was as if they were sitting on cement chairs waiting for their turn at the guillotine.

One of the biggest cases of the firm's career had just lost an important motion in a high profile celebrity divorce case. It's true when they say that bad news flows downhill and that meant to the youngest and most inexperienced attorney. It also meant more work and no sleep to make up for the mistake if you didn't get fired.

Spencer Winston, the founder and brutal driving force behind the law firm, had just finished ripping the young attorneys a new one, and wasn't quite finished yet. Even though he was in his sixties with white hair, a dignified and older gentleman, he was sharper and spryer than any fresh-faced interns.

The conference room door opened a crack, just big enough for a young assistant secretary to poke her head in and interrupt the meeting. She cleared her throat, but her voice seemed to get caught in her speech. She tried again. "Excuse me, Mr. Winston, there's an urgent call from Miss O'Connell."

It was as if a light switch had been flipped; Spencer's demeanor changed to that of a kindly old grandfather. He asked with concern. "Is she all right?"

Relieved at not getting reprimanded for interrupting, the assistant politely replied, "She's holding on line four."

Spencer looked at his group and excused himself, not bothering to apologize for the disruption. The room remained quiet after he'd left.

Spencer entered his huge office that reminded most more of a posh flat than a working attorney's office. He shut the door and took a seat behind his Eighteenth Century desk. He was concerned for Megan due to her mental difficulty of not being able to leave the house. He'd thought it was only a mild setback for her, but she'd seemed to be getting worse over the past few months. Having been lifelong friends with her grandfather, he'd promised him on his deathbed that he'd look after the girls. Somewhere along the way, he'd found himself very attached to them. He had never had children of his own; therefore, no grandchildren either.

He picked up the phone and pressed line four. "Megan, what's wrong?"

* * * * *

Megan was sitting in the vet's personal office, accompanied by Jack along with Keno who snoozed at their feet. She had taken a couple of her prescription pills to try to calm down and balance her feelings of flight and anxiety.

Jack waited patiently with her. He was concerned and still a little taken back at her unstable demeanor.

Megan slowly began, trying hard to steady her voice. "Spence, I'm sorry to bother you."

"Nonsense. You can call me anytime, you know that. Are you all right?" he tried to calm her.

"I'm okay." She began to tear up. "Can you come by the house in the next couple of days?"

"Of, course. You still haven't told me what's wrong."

"Eddie," she began. "Eddie was poisoned and he's gone."

"Oh no." Spencer's mind raced. *Who would do such a thing?* He would get to the bottom of it.

"I'm okay. Please come by when you can."

"I will. Take care of yourself."

"Bye." Megan weakly put the receiver back into the cradle.

Jack hugged her tight. Even Keno stood up and put his head on Megan's lap.

CHAPTER THIRTEEN

The black Ford Explorer was parked in the business district of Monterey, which housed large marina storage units, both permanent and portable. In the moonless night, it was highly unlikely that anyone would notice the dark SUV next to a large, portable storage container.

Two people sat in the front seat, a man and a woman. The distinct glow of a computer screen reflected from the dash along with a few other high-tech gadgets.

There was movement from the cargo area and a dark shadow moved erratically—a large black dog then moved from person to person.

The couple was on a long investigation, like so many times before, but not one that any police department would have sanctioned. It was completely covert and anonymous. In fact, no one knew of their important work behind the scenes to catch murderers, serial killers, and pedophiles.

Unfortunately, it took a kidnapping, disappearance, or even a discovered body to propel the couple into action. This time a teenage girl was missing from the San Francisco area. The local police department had deemed the case a runaway and filed paperwork accordingly, but the parents never stopped pleading in the media that something terrible had happened to their daughter. They insisted their daughter wouldn't have chosen to have been gone this long.

Emily Stone sat somberly concentrating on where the girl might have taken refuge and combed through hundreds of reports and news articles on her laptop computer. It was a perfect spot for her mobile Internet access card that allowed the least amount of interference behind the storage facility. Her dark eyes searched for anything that might give them a lead. She was able to gather more information about the girl, Sara Palmer, and did a victimology profile to find out where she most likely would have met up with disaster. In addition, she worked with the girl's known hangouts, friends, Internet friendships, and ideas as to where a girl of seventeen would most likely go and why.

The investigation was a little unusual for their typical type of case, which usually entailed trailing a serial killer. Something in the girl's parents' eyes drove Emily. Even though she didn't have any children of her own she hoped that someone would have looked for her child no matter what.

"Anything new?" asked Rick Lopez. He never tired of watching Emily work. She would push her blonde hair from her eyes as she concentrated. Her drive was amazing and her integrity was solid.

"No. It's like the trail has run cold. Her friend in Pacific Grove never heard from her but told her that she was coming to meet her. And she was seen in the Monterey area." Emily raised her eyes to Rick's. "Something bad has happened to her." She knew that Rick felt the same way she did but just didn't want to say it.

"We don't know that for sure," he said with some hope, but the odds were against it. He was an ex-homicide detective and everything pointed to the fact that Sara had fallen under terrible circumstances. They just hadn't been able to find her in time; now they were looking not only for a body, but the killer too.

Emily took a breath and said, "Let's listen to local police chatter on the scanner and see what comes up tonight."

"Sounds like a plan."

There was a bark from the back seat.

"Well, maybe something to eat first?" Emily cracked a small smile as she started the engine.

CHAPTER FOURTEEN

The patrol car moved through the clustered neighborhoods on a regular patrol schedule. There was nothing usual or interesting to report. Heavy fog had crept into the area over the past few hours, causing a slight drizzle.

The radio had been quiet with very little activity.

Jack was actually a clock watcher this particular evening and couldn't wait for his shift to end. He had other things on his mind besides crime and murder. He hastily turned on the windshield wipers to a slow intermittent speed because the moisture together with the streetlights and oncoming car headlights distorted his view.

Jack's mind wandered back to the events at the veterinarian's office a few days earlier. He wondered how Megan could have found her way back into his life again. Their lives had crossed paths various times throughout their histories. He had known her when they were barely out of diapers in the small town in Iowa, and then the unthinkable had happened. Megan's father had murdered her mother, and she and her sister had been shipped off to California to live with grandparents.

Jack wouldn't see Megan again until college at San Louis Obispo in California. They had dated on and off until five years ago. She had run him through the relationship gauntlet with mood swings and tantrums, but after they'd broken up he had met Tara. Jack grimaced thinking about how badly all his relationships had turned out.

When he'd seen Megan again, Jack had realized that he still had deep feelings for her. She was going through some tough times and he wanted to be there for her. He was going to play it safe and not expect anything from the relationship, just play it as old friends getting back in touch.

Jack's thoughts were abruptly interrupted by Keno's big head poking through the opening between the front seats, pushing his head closer to the windshield to make sure that Jack could easily scratch behind his ears.

* * * * *

Outside the O'Connell estate, Spencer quietly shut the front door of Megan's home. He was casually dressed in cargo pants and polo shirt. He sprightly took the stairs down to his waiting Mercedes. Within seconds, he revved the engine, turned on the headlights, and drove out of the driveway.

The house remained quiet and dark at the late evening hour. The security light flickered and then went out. It left an eerie and shadowy set stage as more fog seeped in. Even the usual night sounds seemed to be silenced by the weather.

Inside, Megan tossed and turned in her big, ornate four-poster bed. She had many nightmares on a regular basis and rarely had a complete night's sleep without disturbing images in her mind of someone trying to kill her. She whimpered in her sleep, which were actually shouts in her terrifying dream.

* * * * *

The front door unlocked and quietly opened as a shadowy figure slipped in. Darrell had stealthily entered the house dressed in black and he softly shut the door behind him, pocketing his key. He moved through the living room like a jungle cat looking for its prey, touching a few art statues with his gloved hand. He

81

paused to look at the computer equipment, taking a moment to figure out where he could fence it in a hurry for decent cash.

Darrell continued to move through the house and into the kitchen; he took three knives from the butcher block. He hesitated for a moment, turning over the knives in his hands, lightly running his thumb and forefinger down the blade. They were like cherished items in his hands and he had difficulty taking his eyes from them.

* * * * *

Megan's bedroom door opened a crack. She peered through the opening because she had heard someone moving around in her house. There weren't any lights on and she knew that Teresa wouldn't be sneaking around in the dark. She thought she heard someone enter the kitchen, but it might have been just one of her dreams or hallucinations from previous prescription pills.

She could see down the hall into the living room. She squinted her eyes, daring not to move from her safe bedroom, and she could see a dark figure moving with catlike precision. The figure looked more ghostly than like an unscrupulous burglar. She watched the figure stop and touch various personal belongings and art pieces. The dark figure then moved down the hallway toward Teresa's room. Megan carefully and quietly shut her bedroom door.

* * * * *

Teresa slept peacefully on her back with her plush comforter pulled halfway up her body. Her face was relaxed and she looked almost angelic. Her dreams must have been light and serene like all dreams should be.

A large butcher knife raised and plunged deep into her chest. She abruptly awoke with a strangled scream, her eyes wide with terror. She saw and recognized her attacker, which only amplified her shock and disbelief.

Teresa managed with all her strength to whisper, "Why?"

She tried to struggle with her attacker because they were about to thrust the knife into her body once again. The phone on the nightstand along with some books was knocked to the floor. During the struggle, Teresa fell from the bed onto the floor and tried desperately to crawl away.

The knife came down several more times and punctured various areas of Teresa's torso. Her nightshirt was splashed with blood. She tried to move, but couldn't catch her breath.

Teresa stopped moving.

The house fell silent and dark again.

She was alone.

Dying.

She was able to move her right hand from underneath her body. The small cordless phone dial tone buzzed. She tried with every last breath to push the emergency number and finally succeeded.

Within two seconds an emergency operator spoke, "911, what's your emergency?"

Teresa tried to speak. Only a small sound escaped her lips, barely audible. "*Ple...ase help...me...*"

Her lifeless hand released the receiver as the dispatcher replied that help was on the way.

* * * * *

The neighborhood was quiet, there wasn't even a dog barking in the distance. Blinds and curtains were tightly drawn in every home, and most residents were safely tucked in their beds not aware that there might be someone wanting to inflict harm on an unsuspecting person.

One sheriff's cruiser pulled up to the curb and cut the lights and engine. Less than two minutes later, a second cruiser parked behind the first and followed the same example. Deputy Sullivan exited his vehicle and met Deputy Romero.

Deputy Romero asked, "What do you have? Anything?"

Deputy Sullivan shifted his utility belt and turned down his portable radio. "The house is the fifth one on the left. It's completely dark and there's no response from the occupants. According to dispatch, the phone is still off the hook."

"Let's go have a look." Romero followed his partner as they quietly advanced on the house.

Both deputies reached the side of the home and stopped for just an instant to quickly glance in a couple of the windows.

No sound.

No movement.

They made their way to a slightly open sliding door and stopped.

Deputy Sullivan reported softly into the police radio. "Officers request backup and closest available K9 unit."

* * * * *

Jack was watching a couple of mischievous teenagers near a park when he was interrupted by dispatch requesting backup.

84

"Available K9 unit requested at 44327 Third Avenue... possible intruders still on premises."

"Mary twenty-four-thirty...please repeat address."

"44327 Third Avenue."

"Mary twenty-four-thirty responding."

"Copy that."

In shock, Jack returned the radio to its cradle. "Megan..." He turned on the lights and raced to the O'Connells' home.

It didn't take Jack long to arrive at his destination. He had cut all the lights as he approached the residence and pulled in behind the two other police cruisers. He quickly got out and approached the two deputies.

From the car, Keno watched his partner and never took his eyes away from him, sensing it was going to be his turn soon enough.

"What's up?" Jack asked.

"Broken slider and the perp might still be inside. Because of the neighborhood, there's probably more than one," explained the deputy.

Jack went to his car, let Keno out, and snapped on his lead. Jack and Keno led the two other officers back to the open sliding door.

Deputies Sullivan and Romero watched every direction and kept cover for their K9 unit.

By this time, several other officers had responded to the call. Romero pointed to the backup officers to take up the exit locations and set up perimeters. Two officers went to the other side of the house, while the other two went to the front door.

After a few tense moments, Jack held Keno close and his cover officers switched on their flashlights with their guns drawn and targeted at the sliding door. They waited for movement or any type of noise.

They all expected the worst and hoped for the best.

Keno kept his nose to the ground picking up a human scent and stayed low with his tail down.

Jack alerted, "This is the Sheriff's Office! Come out or I'll send in the dog! If you don't surrender, the dog will find you and bite you!"

They waited in the unsettling silence.

Jack glanced back at Sullivan and Romero, giving the nod for them to cover him and Keno. He unsnapped the dog's lead. "Keno, search!"

Keno bolted and padded through the kitchen in a systematic search. He stopped momentarily at a bloody dishtowel on the floor, and then continued his search.

Cautiously, the rest of the team entered and began searching, clearing the kitchen before continuing on through the house.

Deputy Sullivan reported, "Clear."

The others called out, "Clear."

They continued down a long hallway. Keno barked and sat down next to Teresa's lifeless body. Jack moved to the body, careful not to disturb any possible evidence around her. He checked her pulse, shook his head to the other officers. He was relieved that it wasn't Megan, but realized that it was Teresa.

He fought his personal feelings and urges to find Megan. He prayed silently that she was still alive.

A bloody knife laid on the floor next to the body.

The deputies continued their search of the rest of the hallway, bedrooms, and living areas all empty and quiet. The intruders were gone and Megan was missing. They examined and cleared every corner of the estate.

Keno searched through the house and picked up a scent but it led outside through the sliding door.

Jack took his cell phone out of his pocket and retraced his steps carefully to the sliding door along with the other officers. "This is Deputy Jack Davis, we need homicide detectives, forensics, and an ambulance at 44327 Third Avenue."

Keno sniffed the air and cocked his head to the side. He alerted and stopped at a small pantry closet door in the kitchen.

A whimper came from the closet.

The officers took the appropriate cover, guns held at eye level, and began to inch toward the small closet.

Keno barked and wagged his tail.

"Keno, down!" commanded Jack.

Obediently, the dog downed and waited.

Jack inhaled, slid up along the wall next to the closet, put his hand on the doorknob, and opened it quickly. He pointed his gun inside the small space with his flashlight poised. Megan tried to blink away the bright light shining in her face. She was alone, shaking, dressed in a nightgown, and bleeding from her arms and legs.

CHAPTER FIFTEEN

"Megan? You okay?" Jack was instantly relieved she was alive and safe in the closet.

"I...I...saw him and then I heard him...oh, God...he..." Megan was clearly traumatized and could barely talk. She couldn't finish telling Jack what she had witnessed.

Jack helped her up and out of the closet careful not to injure her any more than she already was.

Megan then saw Teresa's lifeless body.

"No!" she wailed. "Teresa!"

Jack steered her toward the living room to sit down. To Deputy Sullivan he said, "Keep everyone out and secure the scene inside and outside."

The deputies retraced their steps and went outside.

Jack managed to keep Megan on the couch while she sobbed uncontrollably, shaking her head repeatedly in denial. He grabbed a blanket from the end of the sofa and wrapped it around her.

Sirens quickly approached from a distance.

Outside there were flashing lights from fire trucks and ambulances that had arrived in the driveway, followed by two additional detectives' cars.

* * * * *

From three houses away, Emily and Rick watched the emergency scene unfold. As usual, no one paid them any attention. They had picked up the police request for backup and K9 unit. From experience, they knew that it was serious, so they decided to take a look to see what they could learn from the investigation. The usual questions ran through their minds.

Was it a domestic murder?

88

Kidnapped child?
Serial killer?

On his computer, Rick was searching the database of the current personnel at the Sheriff's Office. He found that Deputy Jack Davis and partner Keno were the ones who searched the house. They had some great captures on their records and Rick had always liked the K9 officers when he worked as a police officer and detective in Santa Cruz. The K9 teams were easy going, took their jobs seriously, had integrity, and generally really wanted to help the public.

He continued to scan through the personnel and found that there were several possible detectives who might be assigned to this case. Detectives Turner and Preston had their fair share of cases, but their record wasn't that great. Detective Preston seemed to have a reputation for unprofessional conduct. Detective Sergeant Martinez was the senior detective in charge of the Monterey County Sheriff's Office and had a couple of solved high profile cases over the past fifteen years.

Emily was lost in her own searches for the residence owners. She found that the home was in a trust through the law firm Winston, Palmer, Chamberlain, Hayward & Associates and there were two sisters living there. She dug deeper only to find out that there were sealed files on the two women dating back to when they were only small children.

Two unmarked police cars pulling into the driveway of the estate interrupted her thoughts.

Emily looked at Rick and said, "Homicide."

"What do you think?" He raised his eyebrows. Rick knew Emily wouldn't want to leave now.

"Let's just wait and see what happens. There's something more to this."

* * * * *

A paramedic was tending to Megan's minor cuts and bruises. Her cuts only needed some bandages.

Several patrol officers gathered at the front door recounting the evening's events, even though most of them hadn't been involved in securing the crime scene. A chaotic influx of police personnel moved in and out of the estate—too many bodies that didn't need to be there. It wasn't clear who was in charge yet.

A forensic technician skillfully bagged and tagged evidence—the bloody knife among the most prominent pieces. The young man with sandy hair carefully documented the entire scene as best as he could with photographs and quick notes.

The coroner's assistant had already put Teresa's body in a bag and was wheeling her away after just a quick preliminary examination. It was obvious she had succumbed to her stabbing injuries, but there would be more forensic evidence to discover back at the morgue that would help identify her killer.

Jack entered the living room and saw Megan sitting on the sofa as the gurney rolled out the front door. She looked small and lost in the current bustle of the police investigation underway. He was just about to move toward Megan in hopes of comforting her when a tall, casually dressed, blond man approached him.

Detective Roy Turner was a serious detective in his early forties, known for not having much tact or a great case closure rate. His even worse half, Detective Stacey Preston, who worked hard to fit in with her male counterparts, stayed close to her partner and eyed Megan on the couch.

"Jack, you have a minute?" Detective Turner motioned him aside while his partner took her cue to sit down and talk to Megan.

He read from a small spiral notebook. "Your girl here was diagnosed as an agoraphobic after the trauma of her grandparents' death. Both she and her sister inherited a good chunk of change." He took a moment to look Jack in the eye. "Let's see. Megan takes medication for her condition and it has some serious side effects...memory loss...mood swings...possible unstable behavior. Maybe aggressive? And now she gets all that money."

"And?" Jack wanted to punch the detective in the face but remained calm.

"Kinda unstable, ain't she, Jack?" He smiled as he dramatically finished with a southern twang. "That why she dumped you five years ago?"

"If you want to know anything else, I suggest you read my report."

"Deputy Jack Davis *saving* the world," sneered the detective.

"At least I try." He turned to leave.

"What else haven't you told us?" The detective watched him closely.

"That you're an asshole, but you already knew that, right?"

Detective Turner frowned as Jack left the room.

There was a small commotion at the front door when Spencer Winston entered through the foyer. "I am her attorney. Miss O'Connell needs to see a doctor right away and she is not in any condition to speak with anyone. Take away some of these meandering deputies to keep the idle gossip to a minimum…"

Detective Stacey Preston was trying her best to be friendly and personable.

"Did you and your sister have a fight?" Preston asked.

"What?" Megan answered, seemingly confused.

"Was it over money or boyfriends?" The detective was trying her best to get some type of confession or at least an admission of guilt.

Megan slowly said, "I don't know what you're talking about. My sister was murdered by that man."

Spencer pushed his way to Megan. "Megan, don't say another word."

"Oh, Spence." Megan hugged him tightly.

"We'll get through this," he assured her.

Detective Preston stood up and barked orders. "Get this man out of here."

"I have every right to be here." Spence stood his ground.

"You're interfering with a crime scene investigation," the detective seethed.

"I'm Megan's attorney. I suggest that if you have any more questions like that, it will be at the police station tomorrow in my presence."

Detective Preston backed down, hating everything about the pompous lawyer. "I think we have enough for now. We'll be in touch." She gave Spencer a look of disgust before she reported back to her partner.

Two members of the forensic services returned from the back bedrooms with more bagged evidence that included clothing and personal articles from both Teresa and Megan.

CHAPTER SIXTEEN

The air was cold and the fog moisture made a crackling sound in the trees as it dripped from leaf to leaf. That didn't stop the search. There was a distinct scent of the target up ahead. It was only a matter of time now before he would find him hiding.

Waiting.

Where he would be finally revealed.

A slight breeze blew past his face and the scent was even stronger, more pronounced.

Through a grove of trees, several downed trunks were lying on their sides from the past several seasons.

The overgrown brush and dry leaves crunched beneath his feet. Some spots of the makeshift path were soft, causing him to sink a little bit, but still, he moved on in a systematic pattern honing in on the scent.

It was almost in front of him.

He knew it was going to be any moment now.

Standing on top of a fallen log, he looked down and there he was hiding.

The regal German shepherd barked, alerting his partner to his find.

Sergeant Alec Weaver stepped forward and rewarded the dog for a job well done. "Good boy, Sam."

A young man stood up from his hiding spot and said, "Wow, I think that was Sam's fastest find time ever." He brushed leaves off his jeans and his Sheriff's Office sweatshirt.

"It's the wind. It's blowing right at him and makes it easier to track your scent out here," Weaver replied.

They walked back to the main field area of K9 training where several off-duty K9 officers worked their dogs through obedience, tracking, and protection work. There were other police volunteers that helped with training as decoys in bite suits, and monitoring the tracking for narcotics detection.

One of the working dogs, a large German shepherd, barked and growled. Massive fur, white teeth, and dark eyes were what drew the eye to this magnificent dog. It was all that he could do to wait for his handler's command.

At the other end of the fenced training area, a volunteer trainer was geared up in a full body bite suit. He moved slightly from side to side and looked more like a Claymation cartoon. The handler yelled out his command in German and the dog took off at lightning speed.

At top speed, the dog took one last bound before he pushed off and jetted through the air, clamping his jaw hard on the shoulder, and taking the decoy down to the ground. The dog continued to pull the trainer, clamping down a couple more times to get a stronger hold.

The handler yelled again for the dog to come off the bite. Instantly the dog let go and trotted back to the handler, who then gave the dog his reward toy.

In another area near a small makeshift building and an abandoned car, three dogs were taking turns finding the hidden narcotics. The systematic search was evident when each dog took its turn. One of the dogs could find the drugs almost immediately, while the other two took a more roundabout route to the final find.

A black truck pulled up in the parking lot next to Jack. Deputy McPherson got out dressed in jeans and an Eighties rock-n-roll t-shirt. His dog, Booker, happily barked and wagged his tail furiously. McPherson walked around to the truck bed and pulled out a large box of canned goods for the homeless.

He gave the box to Jack. "Hey, here you go, just like I promised."

"Thanks." Jack put the box into the back of his truck.

"I don't know how you do it," McPherson said and smiled broadly. "Caped crusader by night and humanitarian by day. I get tired just thinking about it."

Booker and Keno began barking at one another.

"How's it going?" Jack asked. He was a little preoccupied as he looked in the direction of several police officers talking to Deputy Rominger.

"Forget him." McPherson knew his friend was annoyed and angry by the fact that one of his coworkers was now shacking up with his ex-girlfriend.

"I just don't get it." Jack was still in some denial.

"What's there to get? Some women like being treated like shit, that's why they always go for guys like him."

Jack's tone was sarcastic. "Oh, that's why you're still single."

"That's hurts, man. Really hurts." He smiled.

"I'm single now," Jack said. He tried to sound upbeat.

"That's not what I hear." McPherson's face had a look of curiosity.

"What are you talking about?" Jack was annoyed again with the gossip throughout the department.

"Some of the guys were just talking."

"About what?" Jack demanded. He could feel the other officers talking about him behind his back. He'd had to deal with gossip in general, but when his girlfriend had moved out and moved in with Deputy Rominger, it had just made him fume.

"They don't have anything interesting going on in their lives, so they talk. Blow off steam."

"About what?" Jack kept his friend's gaze; he wasn't going to let him off that easily.

McPherson realized that maybe he shouldn't have said anything. "They were just saying that you have the hots for that little space case involved in that homicide."

Taking a deep breath, Jack explained, "We were friends as kids. How do you think that felt seeing a friend dead and the other traumatized?" He turned to let Keno out of the truck. "I think everyone needs to get a life."

CHAPTER SEVENTEEN

The historic bar was located on one of the oldest streets in downtown Monterey. It still resembled an old town during the 1880s with some of the original buildings and antique decorations, and was a favorite hangout for police officers and anyone who worked at the courthouse. It wasn't the destination spot for tourists, but on occasion they would wander inside to check it out.

Inside, the original mahogany antique bar stood the test of time with many worn tables and booths surrounding it. It immediately transported patrons into another earlier, and much gentler, era. There were two antique pool tables at the back alongside some modern dartboards.

The walls were covered with vintage photographs, including early views of Monterey, Carmel, and vista panoramas of California. There were many photos of police officers from the early 1900s to the present, both actual officers and movie portrayals. Newspaper headlines announced police officers killed in the line of duty, LAPD scandals, and cop blockbuster films provided for an interesting read.

There was a black and white snapshot from the era of the Vietnam War depicting a smiling young man barely twenty years old with a German shepherd. It was Sergeant Weaver and it was apparent that his love for his country and working dogs had always been ingrained in him.

Loud voices came from the back of the bar. Three off-duty police officers, including Deputy Rominger, were playing quick games of 9-Ball, while placing bets on the sidelines, their voices getting louder with each turn. With every crack of a break, the balls flew around the pool table. Beer flowed freely as well. It was a time for police officers to let off a little bit of steam and enjoy themselves without worrying about crime and criminals.

Several couples quietly talked at the various booths. Three retired detectives nursed their mixed drinks at the bar. There were a couple other patrons mixed in with the law enforcement community.

Deputy McPherson and Sergeant Weaver ordered their second bottled beers and munched on fried chicken wings. McPherson had just stuffed some chicken in his mouth when he asked, "Have you decided where you're going to take Claire on your vacation?"

"I made the mistake of getting some brochures for her to look at," Weaver said and rolled his eyes.

"She'll have you in a mud bath at some alternative spa where you don't know if they're guys or girls working there." McPherson laughed.

Deputy Rominger yelled loudly from the back of the bar, clearly having downed many drinks.

Ignoring the outburst, Weaver replied, "Don't give her any ideas. She wants to go to Florida."

"That could be fun. Go around spring break time."

Jack entered and approached the bar.

"Hey." McPherson patted his friend on the shoulder.

Jack slowly said, "Sorry about yesterday."

McPherson shrugged. "Already forgotten."

The gray-haired bartender waited patiently with his hands resting against the bar, even though he knew what almost everyone's favorite drink was going to be.

Jack ordered. "Becks. Thanks."

"How's Keno?" Weaver interjected. "Don't let him get stressed with all the calls you've been handling lately."

The bartender set down the bottle of beer. The chilled bottle began to sweat.

"He's doing just fine," Jack said, thinking that it would be nice to have a little relaxation before anyone started in on him again, either about his relationships or his dog.

Rominger had spotted Jack and left his pool game to make his way to the bar. With a little slur—and some definite sarcasm—in his speech, he said, "Thought you'd be at one of those trendy bars up town by now."

"Give it a rest, Blake," McPherson scoffed.

"Maybe you should think about going to a shrink about your problem?" Rominger wasn't going to let Jack off the hook without making his point heard throughout the entire bar.

Jack took a drink of his beer, never looking at Rominger. He knew where this conversation was going to end up. He asked the question for which the deputy was setting him up. "What problem is that?"

"Not being able to satisfy a beautiful woman." Rominger laughed heartily.

Almost on cue, the entire place became quiet with tension in the air. It took two seconds for Jack to grab Rominger by the shirt collar and press him up against the wall with his elbow at his neck.

Two framed photographs fell to the floor.

Jack forcefully said, "Guys like you skate through life leaving a trail of shit behind."

McPherson jumped up. "He isn't worth it, Jack."

Rominger managed a smug smile. "Did I say something wrong?"

"You think that you have all the answers." He pushed harder against Rominger. "Stay away from me. Understand?" He then released his grip on the deputy.

"I'll do much better than that." Rominger made sure he had his balance before he effortlessly uppercut Jack squarely in the jaw.

Jack fell backwards and knocked over a chair.

The fight began.

Two barstools overturned as Rominger got the upper hand on Jack. They scuffled and each took a few well-placed punches. Emotions were high and gaining momentum.

Sergeant Weaver decided he had better intervene before he lost two good cops to suspension. He may have been one of the oldest cops at the department, but he was just as strong as any of the rookies. He pulled Rominger off Jack. "Knock it off!"

McPherson put his body in between Rominger and Jack. "Okay, we've seen that you both aren't just bad asses but assholes too."

Rominger wiped the blood from his lip, willing Jack to try again. "C'mon, let's go, stud."

McPherson pushed Rominger toward the pool tables and followed him.

Jack picked up a bar stool and sat down to finish his beer that miraculously hadn't been knocked over during the altercation.

Weaver asked, "Feeling better?"

"Much."

Returning to the previous subject, the sergeant asked, "How's Keno?"

"He's been doing great. He hits on everything he's supposed to, and he comes off his bites perfectly, despite your reservations about him being a Lab."

"I know." Weaver smiled.

"I think he's the best damn dog the department has ever had." Jack was exhausted and completely tired of having to explain himself all the time.

"I know." Weaver was amused watching Jack stand up for his four-legged partner.

Jack looked at his sergeant and softened. "You know?"

"Keno has so much potential, *especially* for a Lab." He laughed and paused as two people walked by them. "I will be retiring in sixteen months and I'm going to put in a good word for you to be promoted to sergeant and take over the K9 unit."

"I'm sorry for the attitude lately," Jack said, taken back. "It just hasn't been my week."

"Just keep it under control. This thing with Blake will blow over."

"I know," Jack replied slowly. He knew that time was the only medicine.

Weaver lifted his beer in the air. "Here's to our partners."

Jack added, "Our silent partners."

They clinked their beer bottles.

CHAPTER EIGHTEEN

The door to the Monterey County jail administrative building opened and Johnny quickly rushed down the stairs passing several off-duty police officers. He took two stairs at a time and swiftly hit the sidewalk. He was so glad to be bailed out of jail after what he had been through the past few days. He still couldn't believe that Don was dead.

Johnny had spent more of his adult life behind bars; the taste of freedom had never been as fine as it was today.

Many ideas ran through his mind, from how he was going to commit his next crime to how many ways he was going to make the cops pay for what they had done to his friend. A mania took over his subconscious as a continuous loop played in his head.

Johnny walked through the parking lot and made his way to the street. He turned right and began walking as instructed down the sidewalk. Excitement filled him as he thought about his newest job with Darrell. He felt a renewed sense of worth, even if he didn't know exactly why he felt that way or what was in store for him.

A new model silver Mercedes sedan eased up alongside Johnny and the passenger window slid down. "Get in," Darrell said flatly.

Johnny promptly got in the sleek European car, impressed and relieved that Darrell was there to pick him up. "Styling wheels, man," he said.

"It's fair."

The car pulled away from the curb and headed south. The traffic was light and several sheriff patrol cars passed them on their way back to the department.

"Fair?" He gaped at his boss. "Man, this is nice. I could see myself driving this kind of car. What do you think?" He ran his hand over the dash. "Maybe after this big job goes down?"

"Sure, why not."

Johnny watched more cop cars drive past them. He craned his head to watch them drive on down the road. "Doesn't it bother you being around all these pigs?"

"They can't catch me." Darrell remained calm and in control. He didn't allow himself to feel any fear or apprehension.

"Where are we going? Johnny asked.

"To get you fitted for the next job."

Johnny leaned back in the comfortable seat and smiled. "Cool."

They drove south for about twenty-five minutes to a rundown part of town. The city was trying to update and condemn old apartment complexes. It was a sad state of affairs, but some neighborhoods didn't support the progressive approach of societal rules. There was a housing complex that had been abandoned except for gang members or drug users to occupy.

Darrell pulled the car around back and out of the way from any prying eyes. He didn't want his stolen car to be stolen again by some opportunistic teenager looking for a joyride or a race. He parked the car just out of view in an ally. It was only going to take a short period of time to get everything set up.

Both men got out of the car.

Johnny eagerly followed Darrell down the ally and through a squeaky wrought-iron gate. Darrell jimmied the lock of a door leading into the abandoned apartment building.

Both men entered through the doorway and began to ascend a rickety staircase with several railings missing. Gang graffiti with all its colorful identification and warnings covered the walls. Layers of garbage covered the floors. The air smelled moldy and stale.

Johnny prattled on about unimportant things as they climbed more stairs. He said, "This time things are going to be different. We are going to retire to the islands." He took a moment to catch his breath. "Right, Darrell?"

"Sure."

"We can afford to buy giant houses and pay people to wait on us."

Darrell followed Johnny and had other thoughts on his mind. He had no use for chatter and pipe dreams; he was rooted in reality.

Johnny stopped and turned around. "Right, Darrell?"

Darrell didn't say anything.

The darkened hallway led down to an elevator that waited; it was open like an abyss.

Johnny's eyes tried to focus on the hallway.

The air was stuffy and had become warmer than on the previous floors.

"What's the next job?" he said a little nervously.

"It's right here," Darrell calmly explained.

Johnny took another step and looked around. "What do you mean? Where?"

Darrell took a step toward him.

"I don't understand," Johnny said.

Slowly, Darrell took a long, thin knife from his pocket. "Don't you get it?" He began to laugh.

Trying to laugh too, Johnny said, "No really...where's the job?"

With a quick flick of his wrist, Darrell efficiently swiped his left hand and sliced the front of Johnny's throat. "You screwed up and let the cops catch you." He leaned in close and whispered to him. "You're the job, you fucking moron." He raised the knife to his lips and gently licked the blood from the blade to savor the last living remains of his victim.

Johnny's hands clutched at his bleeding throat. The warm blood gushed over his hands. His mind buzzed and his head felt heavy. The hallway looked like it was ten miles long and getting longer by the second.

He staggered back, eyes wide in terror. With his draining strength, he tried to push on his throat harder in a last ditch effort to stop the bleeding.

Darrell pushed Johnny back farther into the darkness. He smiled and shoved the bleeding man into the dark hole of the elevator shaft.

In less than a second, Johnny hit the bottom with a dull thud. He knew that Johnny was probably dead before he smashed every bone in his body. Pity, he thought, that he didn't get to hear him writhe in pain before the end.

Darrell had stashed a couple of gasoline cans in the hallway underneath some garbage and poured the contents down the shaft to the grave below. With an unnerving calmness, he lit a cigarette, took a couple of puffs, and exhaled with exhilaration. With his thumb and forefinger, he masterfully flicked the smoldering butt over his right shoulder and it disappeared into the darkness.

Smoke began to rise and flames ignited from the bottom floor, growing to large, out of control flames.

Darrell quickly jogged back down the stairs to the entrance. Smoke billowed from the lower floors out the windows. He stood for a moment to enjoy the view and to feel the heat and bask in the gray smoke of death. He ran his pinky finger over the blade once again, still tasting Johnny's blood on his tongue. He wanted more.

CHAPTER NINETEEN

The words ran though his mind a hundred different ways and none of them seemed to be right. He rehearsed some things in his truck on his way over, but everything seemed stilted and contrived. Basically, he thought he sounded stupid.

What is this so difficult?

Why am I having this much hesitation?

He just wanted to know how she was doing and he was just being friendly—he was being a friend, that's all.

Standing awkwardly at the front door of Megan's estate, Jack rubbed the back of his neck and took a step from side to side. If someone were watching him they would think that he needed to use the bathroom instead of trying to figure out what to say. He was a cop—a seasoned cop. He had taken down murderers, been in shootouts with local gang members, and had seen his fair share of crime, gore, and murder.

What is my problem?

He looked back at his truck where the windows were being fogged up by Keno and Tina. The truck shook a little bit from their furiously wagging tails. They wanted out by any means. *They always know what to do*, Jack thought dryly.

He pushed the doorbell button and waited.

Slowly the door opened, and Megan blinked in surprise to see Jack standing there. She was dressed in jeans and a pale pink t-shirt. Her feet were bare and she wore just a hint of makeup to bring out her dark, soulful eyes.

107

"Jack. It's nice to see you." She waited, her eyes watching him closely.

There was an awkward silence.

"Did I catch you at a bad time?" Jack finally asked. *Lame*, he thought.

"Not at all." She couldn't quite meet his gaze. "Any news about my sister?"

Jack felt bad. He had been so wrapped up in how he was feeling that he didn't even take into consideration that she was going through something that he couldn't even imagine. "I'm sorry." He shook his head. "I wanted to see how you were doing."

"Managing," she said weakly. She then noticed the two dogs in the truck. "Your backup?" She forced a weak smile.

"Always." He felt awkward standing there, but still wanted to tell her how he felt.

"Why don't you bring them inside and I'll make us some coffee." She opened the door wider.

"Better make it decaf for Keno...he's already too wired."

Megan laughed. "Just water then."

Her face lit up and Jack remembered how beautiful she looked when they were having fun together. He jogged down the stairs to the truck and opened the passenger door. Both dogs bolted, ran past him almost knocking him to the ground, and then bounded up the stairs to greet Megan. Running in circles, each dog took turns greeting her properly.

"Aren't you both beautiful." She knelt down to pet them as they took turns licking her face. It was good for her to be around dogs during this horrible time in her life.

Jack said, "You know my partner, Keno, and this pretty girl is Tina."

Looking down, Megan said, "It's nice to meet you." Looking at Jack she invited, "Please come in."

The dogs pushed their way into the house first, followed by Jack. Megan shut the door and guided them to the kitchen. She found some doggie treats and filled a bowl of water. The dogs took off and explored the house, making sure not to miss anything important. Keno padded back into the kitchen and sat next to Megan as she prepared coffee. She took two coffee mugs from the cupboard.

"Gets a little too quiet around here now," she said tensely.

Jack eyed the knife holder minus the three knives. Personal knick-knacks were scattered around along with some picture frames. In a light wood frame was a photo of Megan, Teresa, and a man with a baseball hat.

Megan gave Jack a cup of coffee. "Still black?"

"Yep." He smiled. "Who's that?" He pointed at the photo.

"Me and Teresa and Tad, her husband." She looked away. "Now they are gone." She tried to busy herself in the kitchen, trying not to show her extreme distress.

Jack picked up a black and white photo in a dark wooden frame of two little girls and a little boy; they were holding fishing poles. "I remember when this photo was taken." He smiled and remembered what a great day they had together.

"We were inseparable. That was a fun summer."

Jack put the photo back down and turned to Megan. "Are you doing okay here alone?"

Megan took a breath and stood up straight. "I'm fine," she replied.

"Have you had dinner?"

"No."

"Would you like to go out for dinner?" He smiled and wasn't going to let her say no.

Megan searched Jack's handsome face. Their eyes locked for a moment and that familiar sexual intensity began to ignite again.

"I don't know," she said.

"It would just be the four of us." He laughed and Megan couldn't help but laugh too.

"I'm afraid that I wouldn't be very good company," she said.

"Can you leave the house?" He put his coffee cup in the sink and realized how rude that sounded. "I mean—"

"I can go outside the house and I promise that I won't freak out on you," Megan replied.

"That's not what I mean."

She touched his arm. "It's okay. I'm taking only one medication right now. I'm feeling much better." She took her coffee cup and rinsed it out in the sink.

"I know a perfect, quiet place with great food."

Keno's ears perked up at the word *food*.

Megan took a couple of deep breaths and relaxed. She smiled at Jack with more focus. Her shoulders lowered and her voice became stronger. She looked around the house with some melancholy reactions, looking at the closet where she hid, glancing toward the hallway, and then she seemed to snap back into reality.

"Okay," she answered and smiled.

CHAPTER TWENTY

The China Café was one of the favorite Chinese restaurants in downtown Monterey for many of the local residents. It had only ten tables pushed close together, but the food was great. It was a cozy restaurant resembling a friendly family environment. A large picture window faced the street and many onlookers couldn't resist looking through the glass at the delicious entrees at the tables.

Parked across the street under a burned out streetlight was dark gray Acura coupe. The interior of the car was dark, but the glow of a cigarette was visible. There was a faint flicker of light reflecting off a beer bottle from passing car headlights.

Darrell had been waiting and watching for about a half hour. It was amazing what you could discover by just watching and paying attention to what's going on around you, he thought. Most people did not even notice what was around them. They were so self-involved in what they were doing.

That was the perfect time to strike.

He watched Jack and Megan enter the Chinese restaurant and they were immediately seated at a window table. They smiled frequently at each other and looked to be on a first date, but Darrell knew the history. He didn't like the fact that Megan was chummy with a cop, but that really didn't matter.

His attention turned to two young prostitutes talking animatedly to one another down the side ally. They were dressed in short skirts and bright florescent, midriff-baring tops. Most people wouldn't notice that they were prostitutes and might think they were just some young girls who snuck out of their houses for a night of fun and adventure. He continued to observe them until an old pickup truck stopped and picked up one of the girls—leaving one girl alone.

Darrell smiled.

* * * * *

Jack poured a cup of traditional hot tea for Megan and himself. There was an awkward silence. It almost seemed like they were on a first date. Megan was dressed in a light pair of jeans, black boots, and a bright pink blouse that showed off her beautiful eyes. Jack remembered that it only took Megan a few minutes to get ready unlike some of the other women he had known who took at least an hour.

"Do you eat here a lot?" Megan asked.

"Ever since they were held up a few years ago." He took a sip of tea. "Just fell in love with the food."

Megan laughed and her eyes seemed to sparkle.

"I like that," he said.

"What?" She blushed slightly.

"Seeing you laugh." He kept her gaze for a few moments.

A tall, thin waitress approached the table. She pulled out her small notepad and said, "Can I take your order?"

Jack asked Megan, "Need more time?"

"Go ahead and order for both of us… I trust you."

"Two number threes, please."

"Thanks." The waitress took their menus and left to put in their order.

Megan looked around the restaurant and saw that there were mostly couples seated at the tables around them. She noticed a striking couple sitting two tables away—a petite, blonde woman with a dark-haired, handsome man. It was obvious to her that they were in love. There was something appealing and solid about the couple, but at the same time, it seemed as if they had a secret— something no one else knew.

Jack turned his gaze to see who Megan was looking at; he, too, had noticed the attractive couple.

Megan turned her attention to Jack. "I didn't know you were a K9 unit now."

"I've been on the streets with Keno for about a year and half."

Megan paused and smiled. "You look good. It definitely agrees with you."

Jack reached across the table and took Megan's hand. "I'm sorry that you've had it so tough. It's more than anyone should have to bear in any lifetime."

Embarrassed and flustered, Megan pulled her hand away. She absently rubbed her forehead. "I just really miss Teresa. It's not the same anymore and it never will be."

* * * * *

Darrell exited his car and took the long way around to the ally where the young girl was eagerly awaiting a potential customer. He approached the young girl, who was no more than eighteen. She wore a short black leather skirt and short pink sweater.

* * * * *

She smiled sweetly at Darrell. She admired the dark-haired man with a goatee—even though he had tattoos—but he looked like he had some money. It was getting colder and she wanted to find a warm place, like a car or motel room to rest and relax for a little bit of time.

113

Smiling pleasantly, she asked in her best little girl voice, "You lookin' for a date?"

"I think that can be arranged." He took a small roll of hundred dollar bills out of his pocket.

She eyed the stash and knew that this evening was going to be a short one. Her friend, Tiffany, was going to be so jealous. Maybe this was her Richard Gere from *Pretty Woman*, she thought hopefully.

* * * * *

Emily and Rick polished off their sweet and sour pork and cashew shrimp. Both were hungrier than they had originally thought and the food was excellent. It was actually a working dinner for them. They had followed the K9 officer and his friend into the restaurant and wanted to observe them covertly. They thought that it was interesting that the cop was dating a murder suspect.

They wanted to know more and why. The sister as the murder suspect seemed to be too convenient for some reason.

This latest murder nagged at Emily because she felt in her gut that whoever was behind it was connected to their investigation. They still had to pick up the trail of Sara Palmer. Her last known whereabouts stopped in Monterey.

Emily remembered back when she and Rick first had dinner in a Chinese restaurant in Indiana. It was such a wonderful evening and the beginning of something so much bigger than she would have ever thought possible.

Rick watched Emily, knowing her well. "That was a great evening, wasn't it?"

"What?" she said surprised.

"That evening in Indiana." He smiled.

* * * * *

There had been so many covert investigations since that night. Rick had almost lost Emily, but now, he was going to make sure that nothing ever happened to her. Her work was too important to too many people. There was two of them now searching and tracking down killers and looking for missing children.

Emily took a sip of her lemon water. She knew that she couldn't keep any secrets from Rick. "What am I thinking now?" she toyed.

He leaned in and whispered. "I'll show you later."

* * * * *

Jack and Megan did an exceptional job cleaning most of their plates. They talked about their lives and when they'd been together. It was a pleasant evening, but Jack couldn't help notice that Megan looked pale and then had slowly begun to look stressed and uncomfortable.

He asked, "You okay? You look a little bit pale."

"I'm okay," she said slowly as she picked at the remaining food on her plate. "I'm just scared, Jack. This is the first time that I have to face everything alone."

Jack stopped eating. "You won't have to face it alone. I promise."

Megan smiled and then the smile faded from her face. She stood up and grabbed her purse. "Please, excuse me." Jack stood too. "It's okay, really," she explained. "I just need some air. It's my anxiety, I'll be fine in a few minutes."

She hurried to the back of the restaurant and disappeared out the back door. Two cooks barely noticed her departure.

Jack could do nothing except wait for her to return.

The back alley was typical of most restaurant alleys with the dampness and the smell of rotting garbage. Megan steadied herself as she walked a little ways away from the garbage dumpsters. Her head felt light and she felt jittery in her arms and legs. Her mind began wandering.

Everything felt surreal and unfamiliar.

She decided to take a short walk before returning to the table.

* * * * *

Darrell emerged from the other end of the alley, kicking an empty whiskey bottle as he rounded the corner. He felt better and wanted to get back to the anonymity of his car. He had more work but still had to have some fun.

* * * * *

Megan returned to the back door of the restaurant, relaxed and calmer, and feeling more confident and in control. She stood at the back door for a moment to regain her composure, smoothing her blouse and fluffing her hair.

She walked through the kitchen, once again unnoticed, and returned to the table where Jack patiently waited.

Emily and Rick subtly watched her return without actually turning their heads to look at her.

Megan sat down at the table a little flushed, but looking much better.

"Is everything all right?" Jack asked with concern.

"Yes. I just have to take things slowly." She smiled brightly. "I'm feeling better."

"Good. I hope it's the company."

* * * * *

A grimy man in his mid-fifties staggered to a dumpster in search of a place to consume his booze, the bottle stashed inside a dirty brown paper bag. He leaned up against the metal side of the large trash receptacle steadying his hand. The evening was chilly and the alcohol would warm him until morning when he would find a better place to rest. He gently poured the drink into his mouth and gulped the contents.

A pink piece of fabric protruded from the dumpster's lid.

Curious, the drunk slowly opened the top. When he looked inside, he gagged in repulsion and then vomited up his liquid dinner.

CHAPTER TWENTY-ONE

Inside the Monterey County Sheriff's Office, several divisions divided the various areas of police work. The energy was bustling with personnel going about their duties. There were both civilian and police workers with important jobs to do in order to keep everything running smoothly and the county safe.

Phones were ringing.

The employees in records and warrants were busy responding to various demanding requests for information on possible suspects, and warrant checks from police officers and detectives.

Patrol was finalizing their reports from the first watch.

The investigative division was located on the farthest side of the administrative building. The division was divided into five distinct areas of robbery/homicide including sex crimes, crimes against property, narcotics, special operations, and homeland security.

Detective Preston sat at her cluttered desk with a mountain of paperwork. Her eyes looked tired from the lack of sleep. She looked up as her partner, Detective Turner, entered the area with a file folder in his hand and a confident look on his face. He seemed to have a new energy after their grueling last few days working homicide.

"Results back from the lab?" she asked.

"Yup."

"What do we have?" She was getting annoyed with her partner's cloak and dagger routine.

"Pretty much what we figured." He dropped the file folder on her desk.

"And?"

He sat on the edge of the detective's desk. "Megan O'Connell's fingerprints are all over the knife, just hers. And both hers and the deceased's hair on the nightclothes. There weren't any other fingerprints or hair that couldn't be accounted for."

Preston frowned. "Pretty circumstantial. They lived in the same house."

"Maybe." He had a hint of optimism in his voice.

"Meaning?"

Turner opened the file folder for his partner to see the reports from the coroner's division and forensics. "We've got enough to bring her in for more questioning. She's weak and will crumble if we just keep at her."

"Her and her attorney," Preston said sourly. She absolutely hated attorneys, and not just because her ex-husband was an attorney. They just slowed down the judicial process and hindered important investigations.

A stocky man with a moderately thinning hairline wearing a dark suit entered the division. It was obvious he was in charge and, in his presence, everyone seemed to look busier than before. Detective Sergeant Martinez dropped files on various detectives' desks and said his good mornings before making his way to Turner and Preston.

"What do you have?" he said, matter of fact.

"Fingerprints on murder weapon. No other evidence from any unknown source and there was no sign of a forced entry to indicate it was a break-in like the victim's sister said," Turner informed.

"Bringing in the sister for questioning?" The detective sergeant shifted his weight slightly and eyed the detective team.

"Yes," said Turner. "We're on our way."

"Good. I look forward to your report." The detective sergeant left the two detectives and went to his personal office to answer phone messages.

Turner's cell phone rang. He pressed the answer button and turned slightly away from the conversations around the room. "Turner." He listened. "You sure?" He smiled and nodded at his partner. "Thanks." He ended the call and slipped the phone into his suit's breast pocket.

"What's up?" Preston hoped she was going to have a better day than yesterday.

"Another murder weapon," he said.

CHAPTER TWENTY-TWO

Two tattered brown and green reclining chairs dominated the small apartment living room. A scuffed wooden coffee table was covered with shell casings of various calibers. There were several ammunition boxes and military supplies stacked in one corner. A worn walkway through an outdated gold shag carpet led into a small, grungy kitchen.

Rap music played from a portable CD player on the counter with the volume turned to low. Two men's voices interrupted the pounding repetition.

Darrell sat at a small fold-out kitchen table facing a man in military fatigues wearing a black baseball cap. Numerous fast food wrappers and an overflowing ashtray covered the tabletop along with two Glocks, three Berettas, and several loaded clips.

Darrell said, "We just have to sit back and wait for those stupid cops to do their jobs."

The other man lit another cigarette and took a long drag. He lingered a moment, savoring the taste—this man was Tad Brooks, Teresa's supposedly dead husband. Alive and well.

Tad looked at Darrell and replied, "I can't take that chance."

"What do you mean? I need money." Darrell was beginning to panic. He wanted to get out of town and finally live the good life.

"She needs to be put away for a long time one way or another. And that's going to take a little time to execute the plan," Tad explained.

"It'll happen."

Exhaling smoke, Tad said, "I've been waiting a long time for that money, setting up everything perfectly. I don't want any mistakes now."

"You know me, man. I'm totally on it."

Tad looked at Darrell and kept his stare. "If you weren't my brother, I'd put a bullet right here." He pressed his forefinger against Darrell's forehead.

Darrell tried to ignore his brother's antagonistic action, but the truth was he was scared of him, and what he might do at any time. His hands slightly shook as he picked up a Glock and inserted a loaded clip and then took aim at an inanimate object.

"Just let me dust the Megan bitch. She's all that stands in the way of our future."

Tad exploded. "Don't you see that would raise suspicion when I come back into the picture?!" He regularly reminded his brother about his impulsivity. "If Megan gets committed for being insane and for killing her sister, then the cops won't be looking to me. Who the fuck cares, right? All the money then is mine as I come back into the picture suffering from some form of amnesia. I will be the only living relative in charge of the estate."

"I guess," said Darrell, looking down at the floor.

"What do you mean, you guess?" Tad grabbed Darrell's hand holding the gun and forced the barrel under his jaw, overpowering him easily. "You better not screw this up! There's way too much money at stake. Understand me!"

"Okay."

"Understand me?!" He pressed the gun harder into his brother's neck.

"Yes! Please put the gun down." Darrell stared at the dark look in Tad's eyes, knowing his brother could kill him as if it was business as usual.

The vein in Tad's neck bulged and he instinctively began to squeeze the trigger. He eyed his brother closely.

"Please, don't," Darrell barely whispered.

Tad released the gun from his brother and casually holstered it in his waistband.

"What more do you want me to do?" Darrell breathed a sigh of relief. He rubbed his neck and watched his brother.

"Just do what we planned. I've got the rest covered."

CHAPTER TWENTY-THREE

Her eyes were open, glazed over with a sickly film, staring at whoever just happened to be standing over her. She was frozen in time forever, but she had all the answers to the most pressing questions.

The frail, lifeless body of the teenage girl was immersed in dried blood. Her last breaths of life were surely that of pure terror. There was so much blood that it had seeped out around the cracks of the tool box and dried in peculiar puddles, making it difficult to walk around the scene without contaminating the evidence.

There was a flash of a digital camera. The forensic technician was documenting the scene from various angles and distances.

Detective Sergeant Martinez examined the body with a gloved hand making notes that the girl had been stabbed more than twenty times from what he could see. The medical examiner would be able to count exactly how many wounds had been inflicted, and which ones had been the fatal thrusts. It was clear to him that she was killed in the toolbox and not just dumped there to hide the body. He estimated that the body had been there for about a week, maybe a little bit less.

The construction foreman was still shaking and visibly sweating as he spoke with uniformed officers and related all the details of finding the body to them for their reports. They had shut down the construction project for a couple of weeks due to the lack of funds. It had gone over budget to remodel the large building in order to make it ready for offices. He wasn't sure when the project was going to resume.

The soon to be converted warehouse had building supplies, lumber, tools, large crate boxes with more supplies, and some precarious looking metal support beams.

A young detective with light red hair and a ruddy complexion met up with the detective sergeant. He had several sheets of paper in his hand. "Sir, I got a hit on missing persons from San Francisco PD. This girl was reported missing more than a month ago and her name is Sara Palmer, seventeen, no criminal record. They'll have to check dental or DNA to make an official ID."

"Damn." Martinez shook his head.

There wasn't any visible evidence left behind, including the murder weapon. This was going to be a tough, if not an impossible, case to solve if they couldn't reenact Sara's last few hours.

The young detective hung up his cell phone. "Sir, we have another one."

"Where?"

"Dumpster behind 2nd street. Same MO and it appears to be a young prostitute."

Martinez hated hearing that kind of news, especially with victims so young. Unfortunately, it looked like there was a serial killer on the loose in Monterey and it was going to open up Pandora's box with the media and concerned citizens. He cringed thinking about the fallout that was going to come out of these cases. It would make his job that much more difficult and the pressure to solve the cases would continue to be excruciating.

The other detective waited for instructions from his superior.

"Take Detective Smyth with you and get over there to secure the scene properly. I'll finish up here and meet you there."

"I'm on it."

Martinez knew that this serial killer was experienced and would strike again before they had a solid lead. That meant more distress for families and friends. He hated his job at times, especially now.

He stood up and spoke to the three forensic technicians. "Search the entire building including the outside for anything that the killer might have left behind. I mean search *everything*. I don't care how long it takes."

CHAPTER TWENTY-FOUR

The small police interrogation room was sealed up tight, without windows or any natural lighting, which made occupants feel as if they were underground. There was no escaping the questions that were fired at you. There wasn't anything to avert your attention, just for a moment or two. It was just the walls that were closing in fast, slowly squeezing that important answer out whether you wanted to give it or not.

Detective Preston paced from one square corner of the small room to the next; she seemed to be preoccupied with her holstered gun, making sure it hadn't disappeared from just three seconds ago. She let her partner conduct the interview, she expressed many times that Megan killed her sister.

Detective Turner took a seat at the square metal table across from Megan and Spencer. The detective's demeanor remained somber and congenial. He gave the impression that he was your friend and was willing to do anything to help you. His sunken eyes possessed plenty of creases that told he would laugh heartily if the moment was right.

He began, "Tell us again about how you found yourself in the closet on the night your sister was brutally murdered."

Spencer interjected forcefully. "Detective, we have been through this story a dozen times now. Get to the point."

"I've told you everything I know," Megan said. She was exhausted and her medication was making her feel a little bit drowsy. She was afraid that she was going to start slurring her words.

Turner fired right back. "Have you?"

Preston couldn't remain quiet in the background any longer. She wanted answers. "Aren't those self-inflicted wounds on your arms?"

"No," Megan said weakly.

"C'mon, now, Ms. O'Connell." She couldn't hide her sarcasm.

Spencer stared directly at Preston. "You're not qualified to ask such questions or make assumptions outside your area."

Turner replied. "No?" He looked from Megan to Spencer and then his eyes remained on Megan's demeanor. "Why would a murderer take the time to inflict these types of wounds before they murdered their sister?"

"I'm going to have to advise my client not to answer any more of these questions. It's clearly harassment. We've been more than cooperative and it's clear that you're not looking for the real killer. You have no case." Spencer began putting papers away.

"Quite the contrary," replied Preston.

Spencer got up and put the folder away in his briefcase. "If you did have a case then you would have already charged my client." He coldly smiled. "These so-called tactics are inflammatory and about as dramatic as a rerun of *Law & Order*."

Megan was beginning to feel a panic attack coming on and the stuffy room wasn't helping her creepy feeling of doom. She wanted to get out as soon as possible and put this behind her. "Please, I'll answer any of their questions. I want to find out who killed Teresa." She stressed to Spencer. "*Please*."

JENNIFER CHASE

Both detectives watched her with curiosity. What was she going to tell them that they didn't already know?

CHAPTER TWENTY-FIVE

A small reading light glowed in the police cruiser as Jack spent some time going over paperwork from the evening's earlier briefing. The radio buzzed on and off with nothing that was interesting or pressing, but of course that could change at any moment. He was parked at a far corner of the Del Monte Shopping Center. It was a quiet area and he could easily exit to get to anywhere he needed to go if a situation called for his assistance.

Jack was studying several photocopied pictures of wanted felons and special notes from the homicide detectives neatly stapled together. He flipped through pages and then stopped on one man.

Darrell's face stared back at him.

This person nagged at Jack. The face was cold and without remorse, and it was obvious that this man would kill his mother for his own personal gain. His rap sheet consisted of assaults, robbery, and he was wanted for questioning in two ongoing homicide investigations.

Keno's tail thumped against the back seat.

Jack looked up as Sergeant Weaver pulled in next to him and parked his cruiser. "Keno, stay." He got out of his car to meet his sergeant. "What's up?"

"Not much. Dead tonight."

"I was about to fall asleep reading the briefing notes." Jack looked at the sergeant curiously. "What's really up?" He knew the sergeant's moods. He had a roundabout way of getting answers.

Weaver took a breath and looked like he was dreading having to say what he was going to say. He slowly began, "I thought that things would calm down a bit, and you'd get over this preoccupation with that girl."

"What are you talking about?"

The sergeant got out of his car and looked Jack directly in the eye. "I have to strongly advise against you seeing her. At least until this investigation is closed."

Jack shook his head. "She didn't kill her sister."

"Maybe, but—"

"But what?" Jack demanded.

"She's involved in the homicide investigation." He leaned against his car. "You know how these things work."

"Are you giving me a direct order?" Jack was pushing the situation to the limit and he knew it, but he felt it was worth it.

"There are some things that you don't know about her."

"Like what?" Jack thought he knew everything about Megan, but there was just a little twinge in the back of his mind that there might be something he didn't know.

"She's been in trouble before." He watched Jack's reaction carefully. "Serious trouble."

"What kind of trouble?"

The sergeant hesitated. "She's mentally unstable."

"Aren't we all?" Jack rolled his eyes.

Weaver explained, "After her grandparents were killed in the car wreck, she spent some time on the street."

"What?" Jack was surprised, not knowing what to say.

"She stayed with two prostitutes for a while and one ended up dead."

Jack went to his cruiser and opened the door.

The sergeant continued, "She was a suspect for a while and then later cleared."

"What are you saying, Alec?" Jack tried with all of his inner strength not to blow up at his commanding officer. He was sick and tired of everyone telling him what he should and shouldn't do.

"All I'm saying..." Weaver calmly replied, "all I'm saying is that you need to back off until the investigation is over. Something isn't right about this case."

Jack turned and stood right in his sergeant's face. Even though he was mad, he still respected his opinion. "Tell me your gut instinct. Do you think she killed her sister?"

A few intense seconds passed before he answered. "No."

"My point exactly." Jack got into his cruiser, never looking again at his sergeant, and drove away to find a quiet place to finish his patrol duties for the night.

CHAPTER TWENTY-SIX

There was still crime scene tape across the main entrance. Some of the familiar yellow police tape had broken loose and was caught on some of the bushes in front of the building, fluttering with the slight breeze.

Emily hoisted herself up and through a broken warehouse window, careful not to cut herself on any pieces of broken glass that jutted out precariously.

She jumped down from the windowsill, and took a moment so her eyes could adjust to the darkness inside before making her way to the front entrance. She kept a watchful eye on anything that she could stumble on in the dark.

Rick patiently waited for Emily to unlock the front door to let him inside. They wanted to see the actual crime scene where Sara Palmer's body had been discovered. Even though their immediate work was over, there still was the task of finding the killer.

Headlights approached.

Rick backed up from the entrance and took refuge behind the building, hoping the person in the car wouldn't decide to drive in and see him hiding.

Emily heard the vehicle approach. She quickly squatted down and rested her back against the warehouse wall and tried not to imagine that she was leaning against a spider's nest or even worse. She could see through one of the cracks in the door that it was a police car approaching slowly. Her heart beat faster as many thoughts bombarded her imagination. She was afraid some of the cops were coming back to the crime scene for more documentation or just out of curiosity.

She knew that sometimes they would check periodically to make sure no one was invading their crime scenes.

How ironic, she thought.

The police cruiser slowed and the lights became brighter, shining directly on the building.

Emily closed her eyes.

The light flashed back and forth for what seemed like an eternity. The car pulled in right in front of the warehouse. In the blinding light, Emily felt that she was out in the open for everyone to see and that she'd have some serious explaining to do with the cops. Everything she had worked for and all the covert investigations were going to be over. She squeezed her eyes tightly closed in hopes that everything would go back to normal again.

Alone.

Covert.

She expected the police cruiser's engine to turn off, followed by the sound of a couple of sets of military boots hitting the pavement, but, instead, the car dropped into reverse and the engine revved. The car slowly began to back out of the parking lot. The lights flashed higher up on the walls and soon disappeared. The cruiser continued on down the road on its routine patrol.

Emily let out a breath, relieved that her secret would stay intact—at least for now. She stood up and unlatched the creaky door with little difficulty.

Rick appeared and had the same look on his face she imagined that she did.

Relief.

Rick said, "That was close."

"A little too close." She quickly shut the door after Rick entered.

Emily flipped on her small flashlight and aimed the beam into the warehouse, scanning from one side to the other and then across the floor. It was perfect because it cast just enough light and wouldn't attract any suspicious eyes from outside.

The huge building was in complete disarray. There were large crates, boxes of supplies, scaffoldings, lumber, and some miscellaneous tools. Not to mention, it was thick with dirt and full of heavy cobwebs around every corner, wall, and window. It was doubtful that this renovation project was ever going anywhere.

"What a dump," Rick observed. "Are they trying to remodel or what?"

"I don't know." She shined the beam on the open toolbox that, no doubt, had been photographed from several distances and had once been the final resting place for Sara Palmer.

"Why didn't they take the tool box as evidence?" she said.

"Don't know…"

"There could be foreign hairs or fluids belonging to the killer." Emily approached the box.

Blood had spilled out through the cracks of the box and dried on the floor in artistic bursts. It was disturbing on so many levels, and hard to believe that much blood had escaped a petite, young girl's body.

Footprints around the scene looked to be those of law enforcement—heavy work shoe prints. It was obvious that there had been many cops simply observing instead of working the crime scene based on the frequency and stances of the prints. Sadly, everyone wanted to witness a horrific crime scene firsthand.

"Why was she here?" Emily said more to herself than to Rick.

Rick studied the area. "She never knew what hit her," he surmised. "I bet she was in the toolbox for some time before she was killed."

"From everything we have found out, she was out on the street selling her body. Why?" Emily had a difficult time with where young girls end up because they think that their home life is so intolerable. It never turned out well.

"Could be someone she met at a party or just someone on the street that picked her up," Rick added.

Emily stood up and faced Rick. "I don't like this. There's a killer that's tracking these young, innocent girls because of their particular vulnerabilities."

"A type?" he asked.

"I think it's something that the killer doesn't like about themselves." Emily scanned the rest of the warehouse.

"Maybe something that had been taken away from them, like innocence or loss of a loved one close to them?" Rick suggested.

"That's what I'm thinking, but I need to see the other dumpster crime scene." She was ready to leave the warehouse and didn't care to return any time soon.

"Let's wait until it's a little bit later," said Rick. "We don't want a repeat of being cornered again."

Emily's face clouded as she ran various scenarios through her mind—the types of human nature when it came to psychopaths.

Rick watched her. He knew her too well.

"What are you thinking?" he asked.

"I just can't help coming back to that homicide at the O'Connell residence, the sister. I'm not sure why." She looked at Rick and searched his handsome face for some answer.

"The K9 cop and vic's sister?"

"There's too many unanswered questions. It's a weird situation."

They walked to the main entrance and listened for approaching cars or voices.

Emily turned to Rick. "I think we should stay in town a little while longer to try to uncover leads on who might have killed Sara and also tail the cop."

"I thought you might." Rick smiled and opened the door.

CHAPTER TWENTY-SEVEN

The historical bar was jumping with patrons on a Friday night. There were plenty of off-duty police officers blowing off steam and relaxing with coworkers and friends in a game of pool or darts.

There were only one or two empty chairs in the entire place and it would be packed to full capacity shortly.

Beer pitchers flowed freely.

Burgers, chicken wings, and taco salads were flying out of the small kitchen and being consumed with lighthearted pleasure.

The music volume rose a few levels as the Karaoke machine was set up with the high-tech electronic components.

Jack and Megan entered, looking happy to be together. It felt like old times for them. Jack felt especially good and he'd even relaxed to a level that he didn't think was possible, considering everything that had come to light. It was going to be a fun evening for both of them.

Jack steered them toward the bar next to Deputy McPherson, who was alone.

"Hey, bud," Jack said.

"What's up?" McPherson smiled at Megan. "Hi, I'm John." He politely shook her hand and took a moment to admire her.

"Megan. Nice to meet you," she replied. "You a K9 officer too?"

"Yep. Just me and my smarter, better looking partner." He smiled a big toothy grin and took a gulp of his beer.

138

Jack nudged his friend. "I taught him everything he knows."

"Oh...let's not even go there." He stood up to let Megan sit down. "What are you guys drinking?"

Megan answered brightly, "Heineken."

Jack chimed, "Make it two."

McPherson ordered. "Bartender, we got a match. Two Heinekens, please."

Jack pulled the only remaining bar stool up to Megan and joined her at the bar while McPherson stood between them.

A couple began singing "I Got You Babe" off-key in the Karaoke microphones to a supportive crowd. It didn't seem to matter that they weren't ready to rock a Coliseum as Sonny and Cher; everyone was having a great time anyway.

Jack leaned toward his friend and said, "They can sing better than you."

The two beers arrived.

"That wouldn't be hard," McPherson said, laughing and raising his voice over the escalating volume of the bar.

"Excuse me." Megan jumped down from her bar stool.

"You all right?" Jack asked.

"I'm fine." She smiled. "Relax, I'll be right back." She moved through the bar and located the ladies restroom.

Both deputies watched her make her way in and around the crowds of people.

McPherson stated, "She's cute. Does she have a friend?"

"Not unless she's blind and just out of a women's correctional facility that would be attracted to you." He took a long drink of cold beer.

"That wouldn't be so bad if you think about it," McPherson joked.

Jack began to move toward the Karaoke area.

"It could work out..." McPherson didn't care if anyone heard him or not. He stared at a couple of women walking by. "Hi," he smiled.

In the ladies restroom, Megan stood in front of a flimsy, oval framed mirror. She ran a comb slowly through her shoulder length hair. She took several slow breaths and tried to steady her rising pulse as she tried not to feel so conspicuous and out of place at the bar.

Several women hustled in and out of the small restroom, quickly applying lipstick before they returned to the fun.

A commotion outside was building.

Two women entered the ladies room and saw Megan. One gushed to her, "You're one lucky woman. God, he's handsome and nice. What are the odds with cops these days?"

Megan looked at the woman in surprise. "I'm sorry?"

"Jack."

"What about Jack?" Megan asked.

The woman looked to her friend and said, "She doesn't know." She then opened the bathroom door and steered Megan to see what all the commotion was about.

The audience quieted down. Jack was perched on a bar stool with a microphone in his hand on the Karaoke stage. He looked completely comfortable and relaxed.

The music began to play.

The lights dimmed slightly.

Megan waited where she stood at the ladies room entrance, completely surprised and unable to take her eyes from Jack.

A country tune played, "You Won't Ever Be Lonely" by Andy Griggs.

Jack began to sing as if he had been a professional for years. Couples moved closer together as all eyes were on Jack. Occasionally, people turned as if looking for Megan's reaction.

Megan moved closer to Jack through the crowd. She was drawn to him. It was as if her heart and soul moved her before her head even knew what was happening. She watched every move and heard every heartfelt verse that flowed freely from Jack as he sang directly to her. It seemed like everyone else disappeared in the bar for just a moment. It was a surreal feeling, a wonderful drug side effect that you wanted to have.

Jack watched her move toward him.

She was captivated of him.

* * * * *

A trail of clothes led a path to the mattress on the floor in the middle of the bedroom. Jack hadn't had time to buy new furniture except for a mattress. A white sheet was tacked up precariously with pushpins over the large bedroom window that left a small opening where the evening light dominated.

The room glowed like one would expect in a moonlit garden.

Keno and Tina snoozed comfortably at the doorway leading to the hall. They were in their own doggie dream states.

Wrapped barely in a sheet, Jack and Megan clutched each other closely as they made love. It wasn't like the times before. It was new and exciting. They didn't want to leave each other in fear that they would miss something. Never would they be apart again.

CHAPTER TWENTY-EIGHT

Darrell walked through the Amtrak train station. He watched the few midnight stragglers and homeless through the eyes of a well-rehearsed predator. He could feel immense pressure building in his veins and he couldn't stop his compulsive need even if he had wanted to.

He smiled.

He never wanted to not know what it felt like to be feared, and for his victims to see his face as the last gasp of life dwindled from their lungs. That feeling kept running through his mind and it was what drove him.

He felt small and insignificant when he was around his brother, but when he was out trolling, he was a force that couldn't be reckoned with in his own controlling world of terror. The more he thought about Tad, the more he wanted to kill him. The next best thing was to find a surrogate to take his place.

Calmness washed over him. It was similar to a soothing lullaby that kept his body at bay, while his mind was sharp and alert taking in everything around him.

A young college student who couldn't have been more than nineteen sat in the farthest corner of the station reading a psychology textbook and sipping a cup of coffee. Her long, dark hair was pulled up and clipped. She wore very little makeup and seemed to almost disappear into her baggy sweatshirt and jeans.

Alone.

She was perfect.

Darrell glanced at the times of departures—there was nothing for three hours. He went to the restroom, walked inside the men's and women's, and they both remained empty. It was only a matter of time before the girl needed a bathroom break.

There was a security guard in his early twenties who looked bored and tired. He walked through the main area and then outside and out of sight. He was probably going to have an extra-long smoke break or disappear to his favorite napping spot where he wouldn't be disturbed for more than an hour.

Darrell took a seat several rows away from the girl, allowing him a perfect, undetected view of her. He fidgeted with his hands running his fingers next to one another, so he quickly put them in his jacket pocket.

He waited.

He anticipated the perfect opportunity to show itself to him. There was always a perfect opportunity and that's what made the waiting worthwhile and exciting.

It came sooner than expected.

The girl got up, left her book behind and walked toward the public bathroom.

He stalked her.

* * * * *

Once inside the bathroom stall, she shut the door and flipped the wobbly swivel lock. She took a paper seat protector from the holder and placed it on the toilet seat. Before she could unzip her jeans, the door slammed open knocking her to the floor and took her breath away. She was dazed and bleeding from hitting her head on the metal trash receptacle in the corner.

She looked up confused.

A dark figure stood above her.

She thought she was dreaming at first, and then reality struck her. Anxiety had crept into her mind and body along with the urge to run. It was that little voice inside that many people don't listen to, but now it was going to be too late. She could smell stale beer, cigarettes, and body sweat emanating from the stranger. It immediately repulsed her.

* * * * *

Darrell loomed over her. He had to consciously slow down his heart rate because he would rush the glorious act too quickly if he didn't make himself stop. He took a shiny switchblade from his coat pocket and slightly turned it from side to side so that it would glitter for his victim.

The girl realized her intended fate and began to desperately squeeze underneath the stall in order to escape. She cried out and began working her legs to propel her body under the stall barrier. She managed to say, "*Please, no.*" She begged for mercy with her eyes, lips, and body.

Her pleas only proved to excite Darrell even more.

Darrell loved to hear her voice, but it distracted him too much. Before she could utter another word, he effortlessly lunged forward and slit her throat. He let out a relief of ecstasy as the blade finished the incision. He then took his blade to his lips and sampled the warm blood as she laid convulsing and bleeding out underneath him.

CHAPTER TWENTY-NINE

Megan was tired and found it difficult to focus her eyes on the computer screen anymore. She had been working non-stop for more than six hours for her clients, trying to keep her mind on something besides the horrible things that had happened in her life.

Not everything was horrible. Jack was back and that made her extremely happy. He was always her rock and solid support no matter what happened. She knew that he'd be there for her through anything she was going through. She couldn't help but smile when she fondly thought of him.

Megan stacked various sized papers together and slipped them into the correct working files. She tidied up her desk and put her notes in a neat pile for tomorrow. She had been updating a client's website and blog to make sure that they were in all the Internet search engines.

Her work was satisfying and it kept her mind challenged, but she knew that she needed to get out more to be around people and actually start living again.

She made her usual routine of double-checking all of the windows and doors to make sure that the house was locked up tight. The security keypad was initiated with her special five-digit code.

The house was quiet—too quiet.

She looked around the rooms and began to shut off lights in areas that she wasn't going to be in. She felt a chill and looked over her shoulder again at the darkened areas of the house.

The phone rang.

Megan picked up the receiver. "Hello?"

Nothing.

She said again, "Hello?"

There was a weak voice with static in the background, but it was clear to Megan who it was. Teresa's voice said, "Please make them stop…"

The phone went dead.

Immediately, Megan tried *69. There was nothing, no ring, and no phone number displayed on her caller ID. She was unnerved, but it did sound a lot like her sister. She knew that it wasn't possible, just some kids dialing the wrong number or something, and her mind had just been working overtime in the process of coping.

The house sat quiet as Megan's sleep seemed to be peaceful for once, but she was suddenly awakened by the sound of an incessant tapping against glass. Megan opened her eyes and sat up, fully awake. She threw back her covers and her bare feet hit the carpet. She could still hear the tapping noise—she wasn't dreaming.

Megan moved through the house, quietly and without turning on any lights. She tiptoed down the hallway, bypassed the kitchen, and then moved into the living room. Her heart was pounding and she began to feel her hands sweating. She was scared. She told herself that she needed to relax and concentrate on her steady breathing—slowly in and out.

The tapping slowed its rhythm, but became even louder than before.

Tap… Tap… Tap…

In the dark, Megan stopped in the middle of the living room, unable to move. Her curiosity was just a step away from full-blown panic. The anxiety escalated with a tingling in her arms, wobbliness in her legs, overall shakiness, and the fear of losing control.

She willed her feet to move toward the noise.

The tapping grew louder and slower.

Tap...

Tap...

TAP...

Megan inched her way around the sofa toward the window by the front door. She was mesmerized by the hypnotic sound. She felt like she was detaching from herself. If she stayed inside her living room then nothing could reach her—nothing from this world anyway.

She stopped at the window and pulled back the heavy curtain just as the tapping stopped. It revealed Teresa's anguished face, pale and ghostly, looking in the window.

Megan gasped.

Teresa's image moved slightly, as if begging to come back to this world, but an undertone of evil was present with this imposter posing as her sister. Megan teetered from side to side feeling like she was going to die.

Everything went dark.

Quiet.

* * * * *

Jack was on his usual patrol of the residential neighborhoods, looking from house to house. There was nothing unusual. He knew each yard almost by heart from the amount of times he had driven past. Every pot, bush, and fence in need of painting, he knew from memory.

Keno rested in the back seat; obviously, nothing interested him.

The police cruiser stopped at the end of Megan's driveway. Jack reminisced about the times he had spent with Megan. He knew that their time together now was right.

But something now was wrong—the front door was wide open and the house was dark.

Jack parked. He quickly exited his vehicle with his weapon already drawn. Keno's nose fogged up the back window as he watched his partner approach the dark house in serious stealth mode.

Jack tried not to think of the worst-case scenario, but the reality of the situation was that something was terribly wrong. He swiftly moved up the steps to the front door and paused.

He listened.

There was no sign of any forced entry or intruders. He then walked over the threshold and saw Megan sitting on the sofa. It was dark inside and her white nightgown made her look almost like a ghost.

Jack holstered his gun and knelt at Megan's side. "Megan? What's wrong?"

She sat disoriented for a moment. She appeared to not know what was going on around her and she was extremely pale. Her arms were crossed in front of her and she rocked slightly.

She turned to him and said, "Jack…"

"What happened?" Jack looked suspiciously around the room expecting to see someone jump out of the shadows.

"Teresa…" she weakly said.

"What are you talking about?"

"She… she was here." Megan stood up.

"You had a dream."

"She was here," she said adamantly.

"She couldn't have been here," he said gently. "She's gone, Megan."

"But…"

"I'm off my shift in about an hour. Will you be okay?"

"Will you stay with me tonight?" Megan asked softly.

Jack pulled her to him and brushed her hair from her face. "I'll be back in about an hour and a half." He looked her in the eyes. "Will you be okay until then?"

She snuggled up against him. "Yes."

* * * * *

Megan awoke. It was nearly 5 a.m. She carefully moved herself away from Jack's secure embrace on the overstuffed couch. She hadn't wanted to leave the living room and they were sleeping soundly. He continued to sleep and she gently tucked the blanket back around him. He murmured something and then turned on his side away from her.

Jack's uniform and gun belt rested on the coffee table.

Keno opened his eyes and watched Megan, but ultimately decided that the big chair was much too comfortable to move.

Barefoot and dressed in baggy sweats and tank top underneath a hoodie, Megan fumbled in the kitchen to make some coffee. She noticed that there was garbage strewn outside the sliding door.

"Neighbor's damn dog again…" she said under her breath.

She took a large plastic bag from a drawer and opened the sliding door. The sun was beginning to rise in the horizon and it was going to be a nice, warm day.

She began to pick up the disgusting pieces of torn up garbage and put it into the bag.

Megan stopped.

There were droplets of red splatters covering the side of the house. She leaned closer to the house and touched her fingertips to the red substance.

Megan stood up and followed the trail of red dots around the side of the house to the pool area. The neatly covered pool rippled underneath the tarp toward the shallow end.

She stopped and stared at the erratic movement.

There were small waves and a strange gurgling sound working underneath the tarp.

Megan reached her hand down and touched the tarp with her fingertips. She worked the edges until she uncovered a malfunctioning filter.

"Geez..." she said aloud and nervously laughed.

She unhooked the spray filter and walked to the small storage building. She opened the door. She clasped her hand over her mouth in horror and stumbled backward, falling down hard.

A dog—resembling her deceased dog—dangled from a noose.

Megan crawled backwards and then scrambled back to the house. She stumbled again landing hard on her right knee. Her sweatshirt snagged on a plant hook. She furiously tried to get herself unhooked, but tore her sweatshirt in the process.

Megan ran inside the kitchen. "Jack! Jack!"

Jack jumped up from the couch still with the blanket partially covering him. He instinctively grabbed his Glock 19, ready for anything.

"Megan?" He tried to blink himself more awake.

Keno barked.

Megan was hysterical. "Please...hurry!" She could barely catch her breath.

"Take it easy. Slow down and tell me what's wrong."

"Hurry!"

"Keno, stay," Jack ordered the dog and then followed Megan outside.

Megan's momentum and terror carried her small frame outside once again, followed closely by a sleepy-eyed Jack.

The pool area remained quiet and the storage door was wide open. It was empty except for gardening and pool supplies. The dog was gone.

"It was here! The hanging dog." Megan, agitated, looked around everywhere.

"Just calm down."

"It was here!" she insisted.

Jack investigated the storage room and didn't find anything unusual. He looked at the red spatter on the house by the sliding door, rubbed it between his fingers and smelled the substance. "Catsup."

"What?" Megan moved closer to inspect the catsup.

Jack looked around at the garbage. "Probably from the fast food containers and the remnants of old French fries."

"You don't believe me." Megan was a wreck, but she knew what she had seen.

"You've been under a lot of stress," Jack tried to console her.

"This isn't stress. It was real!" she snapped.

Jack went back inside the kitchen still carrying his service weapon. He absently patted Keno on the head, who looked at him with curiosity.

Megan followed him inside. "I'm not going to wait to be the next victim." She went to one of the drawers in the kitchen and opened it. She took out a .38 revolver. "Teach me how to defend myself."

"Where did you get that?"

"It was my granddad's."

"That isn't going to solve anything."

"I'm just supposed to sit here and wait to end up like my sister? They're going to come after me too." She felt it difficult to breathe and could feel a panic attack coming on, creeping up slowly from her chest.

Calmly, Jack said, "A gun isn't the answer."

"Are you going to help me or not?" She stared directly at Jack.

"It's not as easy as that."

"It's straight forward to me." She searched Jack's face for an answer. "You really don't believe me, do you?"

"I think you saw something." Jack was careful in how he answered her question.

"Why would I lie to you?" She felt like she was going to cry.

"I didn't say that."

There was a knock at the front door. Megan walked toward it and said, "Let's just see who that is…"

She opened the front door to Detectives Preston and Turner. Both detectives noticed the .38 in Megan's hand and Jack barely dressed with his police service weapon.

"Cozy," Preston said.

Turner had a folded paper in his hand. "Megan O'Connell, we have a warrant for your arrest."

Megan stepped back, eyes wide, and in shock. She wailed, "No, no, you can't do this! Tell them, Jack, please tell them…" She continued to protest through her uncontrollable sobs as she was led to a police car.

* * * * *

Jack knew that Spencer would bail Megan out of jail, but he was extremely worried how things were shaping up for her. There was nothing that he could do for her right now.

Fully dressed, he began to examine the pool storage building. Nothing seemed to be out of place. He looked up and saw a small window, which had been forced open. By the fresh scrape marks around the edges, he suspected it had been a recent break-in.

Keno sat obedient and at attention while Jack searched around for clues to corroborate Megan's story. He moved around to the left side of the small building. Caught on the back corner at chest level was a tuft of golden fur. He studied it for a moment. It wasn't real fur, but rather some type of faux animal fur.

"Keno, search," he commanded.

The dog quickly sniffed inside the shed and systematically made his way outside to the fence. He stopped. Energetically, he sniffed the ground below the fence and then worked his canine nose up high. He pawed at a slat along the fence line.

Jack examined Keno's alert. "Good boy."

More golden faux fur was stuck to the fence.

CHAPTER THIRTY

Detectives Preston and Turner were still reviewing evidence and photographs taken at various crimes scenes from earlier in the day. Satisfied, at least for the moment, that they had arrested Megan O'Connell, they also knew that she'd be out quickly.

It was faster than they thought—she'd been out in record time.

Turner grumbled over his paperwork. "I can't believe she's out on bail this quickly tonight."

Preston hung up her cell phone. "Same MO for the train station murder."

"I'd better go see what's going on at the lab."

"Meet you back here in about an hour?" she asked. "It's going to be a long night."

"See you then," he said.

Both detectives went their separate ways.

* * * * *

Jack entered the detective division dressed in street clothes and passed the two homicide detectives; none of them regarded one another. He then spotted Detective Sergeant Martinez making his last rounds. The detective had been a good friend to him when he was a rookie patrol cop. Jack had learned how to secure crime scenes properly and was often requested by the detective during many investigations to manage personnel coming and going, or assist forensics if they were short staffed.

"Hey Dan," Jack said.

"Jack. How's K9 life?"

"Can't complain."

"Sarge still giving you a hard time about Keno?" He smiled.

"Maybe just a bit little less." He looked at the photos of the serial homicide investigation. "You working the case?"

"Yeah, they took me out of robbery to take over the homicide cases since I'm the only one that has ever worked a serial case." He looked at Jack closely. "What brings you here on your night off?"

"You think they found the killer?"

The detective sized him up. "You mean your girlfriend?"

Jack felt small and uncomfortable. He actually felt like he was the one being investigated under a microscope, but he trusted Martinez.

"It's okay." The detective then motioned to Jack to an empty office at the end of the hall. He quietly closed the door.

Jack said, "There was another vic?"

"At the train station."

Jack sat on the corner of the desk, thinking, and troubled by the chain of events. He couldn't figure out how or why Megan was involved in this mess. "Don't you think that the sister's murder was a little too contrived? Convenient?"

"You think she's being set up?" Martinez asked with a flat tone.

"It's just that things don't seem to add up and there are some strange things going on."

The detective liked Jack and he always had. He didn't let many people in to see his so-called softer side. "Then the question to ask is what lengths will the *real* killer go to prove that she is the murderer?"

Jack looked down. "I hate sitting around waiting."

Martinez casually went to the computer at the desk and punched up a couple of letters on the keyboard. He then said with dramatic emphasis, "Suddenly I'm very, very hungry. I'll be gone for forty-five minutes for dinner." He paused at the doorway and continued, "It's amazing what you can come up with when you set your mind to it." He shut the door leaving Jack to stare at the computer screen.

* * * * *

A green Mercedes eased into the driveway of the O'Connell estate. Megan slowly got out, shut the car door, and sprinted up the steps to her front door. She turned and waved before entering her house.

The Mercedes drove away.

Megan was exhausted. She didn't know that she could feel this tired and emotionally worn out. She hadn't had anything to eat all day and she was famished. It was difficult, but she was going to try not to worry about her problems, even though she could be found guilty of murdering her sister.

Life was scrambled up in pieces around her, not just in her mind.

She flipped on the small television on the kitchen counter as she rummaged through the refrigerator and then settled on a bottle of wine. She poured herself a glass.

The news was on and the Sheriff was giving a press conference. He was tall, thin and had silvery hair. He spoke with confidence and compassion. "We are conducting an intensive investigation and have all of our best detectives working these cases."

Megan sipped the wine.

The Sheriff continued, "We have several leads and won't rest until the killer is brought to justice. It is my duty as a public servant to warn any woman not to travel out at night alone, or if you absolutely must, please keep to public and well-lit areas—"

Megan had heard enough and turned the television off.

A soft scraping noise filtered through the wall just on the other side of the kitchen.

Megan moved to the kitchen sliding door as she steadied her weary body against the counter. The room spun from her nervous energy. She turned and looked at the phone, contemplating what to do. She decided to flip the lock on the sliding door to take a look at where the noise was coming from.

She leaned outside and surveyed to the left and then the right, while keeping her feet firmly fixed inside on the floor. Her breath stayed trapped in her lungs as she dared to put a single toe outside.

A familiar voice said, "Meggie?"

Megan turned to the left and let out a noisy exhalation of air. Her eyes acknowledged what she saw. It was her sister standing there in the darkness—waiting.

A strong hand clamped a white cloth over her nose and mouth.

* * * * *

Jack pounded away at the keyboard for more information. He wasn't quite sure what he was looking for, but kept searching because he only had a little more than half an hour.

The computer screen read:

Raymond and Dorothy O'Connell deceased. Raymond died in prison only three years after he murdered his wife. Living relatives are Teresa Brooks and Megan O'Connell. Teresa changed her name when she married.

Jack scratched his head and typed: *Brooks.*

He waited for the results. The computer scrolled out information and a photograph:

Tad Brooks...married to Teresa O'Connell 2003, military special ops, deceased 2010.

Jack looked toward the door. He could hear voices near the office and then they moved down the hall. He continued reading Tad Brooks' death certificate on the screen:

Hiking accident, Sierra, Nevada. Body never recovered.

Jack had seen enough and was almost out of time. He quickly switched off the computer screen. When he stood up at the desk, he knocked a file folder onto the floor. He picked up the folder as his eye caught a name on the report: Spencer Winston; Winston, Palmer, Chamberlain, Hayward & Associates. Attorneys at Law.

The police investigation file contained information and photographs of Jack's fleeing robbery/homicide suspects. One photograph showed Don Campbell dead after falling off the roof. Another mug shot showed Herald "Johnny" Banner who was released on bond by Spencer's law firm.

They paid his bail?

Jack couldn't believe that such a prestigious law firm would post bail on a guy like that.

Scribbled on a legal yellow pad was the name of the third suspect still at large: Monty Stinger. Underneath several binders and file folders was a list of Monterey

County's Most Wanted. A name stood out: Monty Stinger, a.k.a. Darrell Brooks.

Brooks...

Jack flipped the computer screen back on and stared at Darrell and Tad Brooks. There was more than just a family resemblance.

"Shit."

He picked up the phone to call Megan to make sure that she was doing okay.

He waited while the phone rang.

* * * * *

The telephone rang inside Megan's house.

The kitchen sliding door stood wide open.

The house was empty.

The phone continued to ring.

CHAPTER THIRTY-ONE

The San Francisco International Airport was busy with flights taking off in the early morning. Spencer parked his Mercedes in long term parking and got out of his car. He grabbed two carry-on bags and a large suitcase from the trunk. He looked around to make sure that no one was paying any attention to him and that he was not followed.

He unzipped one of the small pieces of luggage to find neatly rolled bills in between personal items. Moving them into hidden compartments, he was sure no one would search him or the luggage. He had done this on so many trips before, but this one was different.

It was permanent.

It was a difficult decision to make, but he was tired of it all.

Everything.

Work. Home. Practice.

He wanted to retire away from everything that he had ever known before. He took the money when it was offered to him the day that Tad and Darrell Brooks approached him. He really didn't have a choice in the matter. As the days went by, the more he thought about it, the more it appealed to him. He had done some things throughout his career that weren't on the positive side of the law, so this was no big deal in the scheme of things.

It was easy to clean out the law firm. He took his time and filtered money from numerous accounts and investments. It would take a forensic accountant ten years to figure out what he really did. Most importantly, he didn't want to be a part of the fraud and murder scheme against Megan.

This was his way out and it was time. He would disappear into South America and maybe Argentina. It was a chance for a new life.

He entered the International terminal and checked his one large luggage and made his way through security with his two carry-ons.

Now all he had to do was wait.

He fidgeted as he waited, absently rubbing his hands together to dry the moisture. He wouldn't feel comfortable until the plane was actually in flight.

The loudspeaker finally announced Flight 324 was boarding for South American Air.

It was time.

There was no turning back now.

CHAPTER THIRTY-TWO

Jack entered the large administrative building of the Sheriff's Department. He was dressed in his uniform and moved toward the desk sergeant on duty. He had received a message that the watch commander needed to see him right away and that wasn't generally good news.

All types of scenarios were tumbling through his suspicious cop mind. Of course, he thought of the worst-case situations like being suspended or booted from K9. Or, maybe someone saw him using an unauthorized computer for his own personal use. There were many options to pick from the past few weeks.

The desk sergeant was generally not in a good mood.

Jack said, "I got a message that Watch Commander Ramsey wants to see me."

The sergeant never looked up from his work. "He's in his office."

"Thanks." Jack walked through the office and down a long hallway to the watch commander's office. He knocked on the door. He heard, "come in" from inside and opened the door.

A distinguished man with gray hair was seated behind a desk, reading over paperwork. He didn't look up.

Jack felt a little bit like he was going to a firing squad. He managed to shift his perception and remained calm. He knew whatever happened, it was already in the works before he ever walked into the office.

Watch Commander Ramsey finally looked up at Jack. It was difficult to read the stoic man's intentions. "Deputy Davis."

"Sir, you wanted to see me?" Jack shifted his weight slightly as he stood in front of the commander.

The commander leaned back in his chair and took off his reading glasses. He made no qualms that he liked Jack, and especially his drive and ambition and that, with him, the department was always number one.

He began, "How's K9?"

"Can't complain. Keno's doing great."

"Glad to hear it. Sergeant Weaver has expressed his recommendation for you to take his place." He watched Jack's reaction.

"Yes, sir." Jack managed a small smile.

"I wouldn't want to see anything that jeopardizes that, would you?" He stared directly at Jack and it was obvious what he was talking about—his relationship with Megan.

"No, Sir."

"Some concerning rumors had been going around the department, and I've always felt the best policy was to go right to the source," the watch commander began.

Here it goes, thought Jack.

An awkward silence followed, filling the room with stifling air. It felt like a standoff. The room was getting warmer by the minute.

A TRIPLE SOUND ALERT from Jack's radio interrupted their conversation.

Dispatch announced, "All available units, please be advised a 411 in progress and shots fired at 2488 2nd Street... two hostages reported..."

Jack was relieved for the interruption and turned to leave the commander's office. "Sorry, Commander, we're going to have to finish this conversation another time."

* * * * *

Megan stirred slightly from her deep slumber. Her mind was foggy and she couldn't remember what day it was or if she had something important to do. She tried to push her way through the murky, muddled thoughts to get to an awakened state.

She shifted her weight slightly and found that her movements were restricted. She opened her eyes, but it was completely dark except for a few cracks of light above her. Her eyes slowly grew accustomed to the dim lighting.

There was the sound of a garbage truck beeping as it backed up. A distant hum of traffic in the distance. There was a rush of emergency sirens that seemed to explode nearby. The sirens followed by hurried voices were somewhere close and she could almost make out what they were saying.

Megan grimaced as she sat up and rubbed her head with her left hand. She needed some aspirin as she began to feel a little shaky without her anti-anxiety medication. The pungent smell of old refrigerator items and musty cardboard entered her senses.

Everything seemed a bit dreamlike and she took a couple of deep breaths to steady herself. She looked down and there was blood covering her left hand. She had wiped that blood across her forehead.

She was clutching something in her right hand and quickly brought it into view.

It was a bloody kitchen knife.

A combination of extreme horror filled Megan. There were too many jumbled questions for her to try and answer all at once.

She became fully awake and realized that she was in a dumpster behind an alley. The dumpster was filled with broken down boxes and used mailing packaging supplies.

A million questions plagued Megan as she tried to climb out of the metal bin.

How did I get here?

Why?

When?

As Megan tried to gain her balance, she flipped the lid open. Immediately light flooded in from outside, and she found that she was right next to a dead woman who resembled her sister.

CHAPTER THIRTY-THREE

More than two square blocks were roped off to anyone coming or going. It was a full-blown crime scene taking on new life with every person that stopped to watch the unsettling events unfold.

Emergency personnel hurried around the perimeter. More than a dozen police cruisers parked directly at the potentially deadly standoff. The streets were narrow and the layers of people and vehicles made it difficult to maneuver efficiently.

One K9 cruiser's entire passenger side was crumpled against a tan Dodge Durango. Deputy Rominger with partner Major were on the street and protected themselves with the smashed vehicle. They were trapped by the events unfolding and they weren't going to let the suspect escape.

Major obediently waited with his handler for a command; until that moment, the Rottweiler had been in the down position pressed up against Rominger's leg.

Several patrol officers preserved the perimeter with guns ready, prepared to use deadly force if, and when, deemed necessary.

A crazed man in his mid-thirties who had taken police on a wild pursuit had now shielded himself with a terrified pregnant woman inside the small convenient store. He pressed his large caliber pistol against her head and then moved it back and forth to her stomach.

The clerk and one customer sat bound against a wall just inside the doorway. The clerk had a fatal gunshot wound to his forehead and the unlucky customer was trying desperately to get his arms free to escape.

On the rooftop were two SWAT snipers waiting poised for the perfect moment and the instructions to take out the dangerous subject.

Sergeant Weaver covered himself with his vehicle as he conferred on the radio about tactical options.

Jack managed to make his way to him.

Weaver asked into the walkie-talkie, "Can we get a shot?"

The response from SWAT Commander was, "Negative."

"We have K9 on standby."

Response: "Use your discretion. Over."

Jack looked to the sergeant. He knew that the situation wasn't going to be peaceful and someone else was going to die if they did not act fast. He had a sick feeling in his stomach, but all of his training was for moments like this. "What do you think?" he asked.

* * * * *

Megan managed to climb completely out of the dumpster. She leaned up against the side of the receptacle to try to steady herself, looking from left to right. Her heart was pounding so hard that she thought she might faint. Everything seemed bizarre and she wanted to be in the safety of her home and put everything behind her.

Another police car zoomed along the main street with lights flashing to assist whatever was going on a few streets away.

Megan instinctively took cover next to the dumpster, afraid of being seen. She looked down at a plastic soda bottle that was half-full. Quickly, she unscrewed the lid and tried desperately to wash the blood from her hands. Using her forearm, she rubbed the blood off her face as best as she could.

* * * * *

Across the street looking through a pair of compact binoculars, Darrell watched Megan from inside a Honda that he had jacked. He smirked as he watched her terrified, trying to make sense of what was happening to her. He was a little annoyed that the exact place he'd chosen to put Megan was the same vicinity of some stupid police standoff.

* * * * *

Megan started to make her escape, but stopped. She had to think and think fast. She reached into the dumpster, trying not to look at the dead woman's face, and retrieved the kitchen knife that she now held so tightly in her hand.

She stared at the long blade for a moment, hypnotized by it as she turned it over in her hands. About a minute later, she tossed the knife into a storm drain where it got stuck only about a foot down from the street.

* * * * *

A couple of cars away from Darrell, a black Ford Explorer sat parked. There was nothing sinister about it, but it seemed to be in the perfect vantage spot to watch several things at once. It was almost impossible to tell if there was anyone inside or not because of the tinted windows.

Emily and Rick sat quietly and watched the two scenarios unfold. They were both still extremely upset by the news that Sara Palmer had been found—dead. It was something that they both had known in their gut, but it didn't make it any easier in reality.

Emily spoke first. "What do you think?"

"I'm not sure. What the hell is going on around here?" Rick saw the standoff with practically every cop on the force involved, including the K9 Deputy Jack Davis. "It's like a circus and everyone comes to town."

Emily smiled. She had to admit it was weird for them to watch the events unfold. She loved Rick's impeccable insight into a situation. "Where is Megan O'Connell going and why is she here?" she asked.

"We need to sit tight." Rick looked over toward the police barrier and couldn't help but feel the officers' anxiety and stress. He had spent most of his adult life being a cop and it still felt strange sitting back and just watching without being a part of it.

"Maybe we can help out." Emily took her SLR digital camera out and began documenting the scene and photographing various parked cars and license plates.

* * * * *

Sergeant Weaver looked Jack in the eye. "Either way we go, it could potentially be really bad."

Jack looked over to Deputy Rominger—despite how he felt about him, he didn't envy some of the decisions he had to make with his canine partner. "What do you think?" he asked again.

"Blake is trained in this type of situation with his SWAT background. He knows how to handle it and what all of his options are. But with Major, I just don't know—"

Both officers could see through the store's window just as the customer had managed to loosen his ropes and escape out the back. It made the civilian an open target and hell was going to break loose if they didn't make some fast decisions.

Weaver exclaimed, "Shit! We have to act now!" Into his walkie-talkie, he said, "Blake, can you see your opportunity?"

Rominger pressed himself closer to the wrecked vehicle as he responded. "I can divert him long enough for the sharpshooter."

Weaver said, "Another problem, the hostage inside the store has made his escape."

"I'm on it." Rominger inched forward and eyed the suspect, taking in everything around him. "Major stay," he commanded.

The dog obeyed, panting in increased agitation.

* * * * *

Megan jogged to the end of the alley away from the commotion and around the corner. Her adrenaline was the only thing that helped her put one foot in front of the other. It almost felt as if she was in a movie, but there were no *cuts* or *action* shouted.

She kept jogging toward safety and away from the crowd. She almost ran right into a uniformed police officer that was keeping the public away from the incident going on at the convenience store.

Completely panicked, she turned around and ran back down the alley toward the dumpster about to head in the opposite direction.

Two gang members turned a corner and saw her. One of the men grabbed hold of her.

"Hey, what's your hurry, baby?"

"Let go of me!" she yelled.

"C'mon, lets party. I got something you'll like." He made a rude gesture toward his crotch.

Megan didn't waste any time and gave a good kick to the groin of one man and scratched the face of the other.

Both men were momentarily stunned by her quick action.

"Ouch! Bitch!" they exclaimed.

Megan didn't take any more time to hesitate and ran around the alley and down the main street. She didn't care if anyone saw her or asked her any questions. She wanted to leave her nightmare behind. Home was the only thing on her mind.

A taxi was turning around to stay away from the crime scene area. Megan was able to make her way to the car before it took off in the other direction. She jumped inside and the taxi took off.

* * * * *

Darrell still watched Megan and smiled as she made her getaway. "Quite the resourceful girl," he said to himself.

His smile soon faded as an ambulance and fire truck stopped right next to him. Paramedics and firefighters began running toward the hostage crisis.

Darrell sat trapped in his car.

He got out of the car, angry. He grabbed the jacket sleeve of a passing paramedic who was tall and built like a tank. "What the hell are you doing? I'm boxed in here!"

"Hey man, relax." The paramedic sized up the intense man dressed completely in black with prison tattoos.

"Relax?" He couldn't believe that this guy had the nerve to tell him to relax. "How am I supposed to get out of here?"

"Maybe you shouldn't have parked there... asshole."

Darrell shoved the paramedic toward the ambulance. Two other emergency personnel stopped and stared at Darrell. They were ready to engage in a fight if they had to.

Angry and defeated, Darrell hesitated and knew he was outmatched and outnumbered. He saw two uniformed police officers rounding the corner of the building, and they were approaching fast.

Darrell retreated, abandoned the car, and then disappeared into the crowd.

* * * * *

Deputy Rominger moved in farther to the store with his weapon perfectly aimed, just as the mad man rested his gun arm down slightly to his side.

"Put the gun down! Now!" He continued toward the armed man. "I said put the gun down now!"

Major was barking non-stop.

A couple of other officers inched their way to secure the narrowing perimeter and to back up Rominger.

The man holding the gun laughed. He slowly put down his gun and loosened the grip on the pregnant woman.

Another customer, who had been hiding inside the building, heroically lunged forward, and pulled the pregnant woman inside to safety.

The man spat out, "I give up...don't shoot...please don't shoot." He kept mumbling apologies repeatedly.

Rominger moved closer to the man, still keeping his gun targeted on the man's torso. "Get down on the ground now! Keep your hands where I can see them!"

Jack, Sergeant Weaver, and several other officers with guns drawn, closed the gap covering the scene until the suspect was in handcuffs.

Jack actually let out a sigh of relief; it was almost over and no one else had to die.

The man was still mumbling incoherently and then his voice turned to a more sinister, sarcastic tone. "Of course, officer...I give up..." He put his hands up. He then slowly got down on his knees in an apparent retreat.

Rominger continued to close the gap. "Get down! Now!"

Major barked, inching a couple of feet forward, watching every move the man made.

The man's left hand slipped under his dark jacket and he grabbed another weapon. He was prepared for every scenario, and he wasn't about to be taken in by the cops.

In less than a split second, Major bolted toward him to take him down.

Rominger yelled to everyone. "Hold your fire!"

The large Rottweiler bounded up to the man, and leaped through the air to take him down as two shots rang out. Taking the bullets fully in the chest, Major hit the ground a few feet away.

An explosion of gunfire erupted. All but a few rounds hit the man in a dancing array of fury, dropping him to the pavement.

Major was still breathing, but badly wounded. Blood seeped through his fur and covered the pavement beneath him. Rominger was at the dog's side. Distraught, he picked up the dog and seemed uncertain of what do.

The other officers were securing the scene.

Rominger looked around for help.

CHAPTER THIRTY-FOUR

Chaos broke out around the shooting crime scene.

Emergency workers and police officers were running in different directions.

News reporters took their opportunity to get footage of the dead man by running into the scene in order to catch all of the gory details for their viewers on TV and the Internet.

Jack appeared at Deputy Rominger's side with a ragged blanket and administered direct pressure to the dog's wounds. He said, "Hold this down! Let's go!"

Jack looked around to find a police cruiser that wasn't blocked in by other vehicles or fire trucks. He couldn't find a way out fast. If they didn't hurry, the dog was going to die.

An attractive, blonde woman dressed in jeans and black t-shirt came to their aid. "This way!" Emily pointed to a black Ford Explorer.

Jack saw that there was no other choice. To Rominger he said, "This way!" He guided him to the civilian vehicle.

As they ran past Sergeant Weaver, Jack yelled to him, "Take care of Keno!"

The sergeant nodded and watched as the two deputies covered in blood ran to a black SUV with grim expressions.

Jack cleared a path to the SUV with Emily. "Get out of the way!" he yelled.

Rominger followed through the menagerie of people. He whispered, "C'mon boy, you can make it."

The dog's breathing was shallow and he was losing blood fast.

A dark-haired, good-looking man met the group at the SUV and opened the back door. He seemed familiar to Jack—he didn't know why, but it didn't matter at the moment.

Rick said, "Hurry, get in."

Jack and Rominger slid into the back seat. Emily quickly shut the door and jumped into the front passenger seat with her big black dog.

Both deputies tried to stop the bleeding as best as they could. It took the strength of both of them to keep the blood flow to a minimum.

Rick jumped into the driver's seat and turned the engine over. It roared to life. It took him only a moment to get the Explorer heading to the veterinary emergency hospital.

He drives with some serious experience, thought Jack.

Rick blew through some signals, but he was still cautious like he had done this many times before.

Rick asked, "Which way?"

"Keep going on Del Monte." Jack took a moment and scanned the car. He noticed that they had quite a bit of computer technology and stacks of reports.

The black Lab in the front seat stared at him during the entire ride.

Jack couldn't help but think about the obvious that it could have been Keno who was shot.

* * * * *

Emily looked at Rick and they were both thinking the same thing. It didn't look good for the police dog. They'd seen the chain of events unfold and there wasn't anyone that could've taken the dog to emergency immediately. They had no other choice, even though their undercover position might be compromised in the process.

CHAPTER THIRTY-FIVE

Tad sat in the broken down recliner and sucked in smoke from his cigarette that was all the way down to the filter. His unsteady hand showed the highly agitated state he was in—waiting. He leaned back with no visible expression on his face, tightening and loosening his left fist.

There were several large ammunition boxes that were open with military explosives and numerous rounds of ammo. Several assault rifles, large caliber handguns, and grenades were neatly stacked in the corners of the living room.

The front door burst open and Darrell barged inside. Clearly angry and he wanted to vent and take hostages of his own. "We've got to get out of here."

Tad confronted his brother. He knew that he must have completely screwed up big this time. "You're not going anywhere."

"What do you mean?" Darrell saw the disturbing look in his brother's eyes.

Tad grabbed his brother by the collar. The vein in his forehead was pulsating. He gritted his teeth as he spoke. "You are staying here. As for me, I'm dead, remember?"

"Tad...man, we're brothers...blood."

Tad softened a bit. "You're right." He let go of Darrell. "We are brothers. Nothing tighter than blood." He held his brother by the shoulders and stared in his eyes. "I love you, brother."

Darrell relaxed and walked to the window and watched a couple of people walk by and then get into their car.

Tad walked up behind Darrell and lassoed his neck with a thin cord and began to strangle him.

Darrell struggled with his older, much stronger brother. "No... please..." His eyes began to bulge and his breath was unable to bring oxygen to his brain. He continued to struggle with his arms and his body writhed in agony with fear of death. No more sound escaped his lips and his legs began to flail, trying to desperately free himself.

"I cared about you, Darrell. I really did care." With a final ravaged tug, Darrell stopped moving.

Tad took the garrote off his brother, his body dropped to the floor as his eyes stared sightlessly at the ceiling. He looked like he was just resting and thinking of something new to do.

Tad knew that his brother was a problem and he was going to kill him when everything was over anyway, but decided that today was the day instead.

The sooner the better. No loose ends.

There was nobody to blame but himself now.

Tad dragged his brother into the bathroom and left him on the floor. There were several cleavers, hacksaw, plastic bags, towels, and some various tools for crushing and breaking bone and cartilage.

He picked up a large, sharp knife and easily decapitated his brother. He tossed the head into the tub.

For a moment, the eyes looked like they blinked and watched him move around the room. Most of the blood would flow down the drain, leaving clean up to be much easier. He then began to systematically dismember the body at the largest joints first, shoulders, elbows, hip, and knees. It was hard work, but he felt a sense of accomplishment as the pieces of his once living brother piled up in the tub to drain.

CHAPTER THIRTY-SIX

The emergency door to the veterinary hospital was still wide open.

The black SUV idled at the back entrance. Rick put the Explorer into reverse and slowly pulled out of the parking lot.

Deputy Rominger leaned up against the back wall inside the emergency room, waiting with Jack. His uniform was completely covered in blood and there were some spatters on his face and neck. He was barely hanging on emotionally and his trauma was obvious from his overwhelmed body language and stress imprinted on his face.

Rominger didn't know what else to do or say, but wanted to keep his mind positive. "I can't lose him. Three years isn't enough." The deputy barely held it together.

"I remember when you got him. What a bite..." Jack tried to smile.

"Yeah..." Rominger said as his voice drifted off.

Dr. Reynolds came out of the examination room.

Rominger asked, "How is he?"

"I've stabilized him, for how long I don't know... he has a few minutes anyway." The vet was somber and shook his head in despair.

The words stung the deputy. He knew it was a mortal wound, but he still had hoped for the best—even a miracle.

Jack felt like he had lost one of the family. It was the most difficult thing that any K9 officer had to go through.

In the examination room, Major's labored breathing lent to his serious condition as he lay helplessly on the examination table. Fluids were being continuously pumped into his system to stabilize him. There were drains that helped with possible infection. The two wounds were clamped off for now to stop the bleeding—the bullets were through and through.

Rominger pulled up a chair and sat at the dog's side, petting him constantly. Major seemed to perk up just by the sight of the deputy.

Jack stood at the doorway, miserable and quiet.

The deputy coaxed the dog and talked to him. "You're going to be fine."

The doctor joined the deputy with more grave news. "I'm sorry, Blake, the bullets pierced through his liver and lung. He won't make it through surgery. The liver is too badly damaged."

The inevitable horror loomed over the room.

"Will he feel pain?" Blake asked.

"No, we give him a total muscle relaxer before the actual euthanasia."

Rominger couldn't hold back anymore. He began to cry. "You did good, boy." He petted him and slowly nodded to the doctor.

The vet gave Major an injection to calm and relax him. Major never took his eyes from his partner.

"It's okay, boy...I'm here..." Rominger barely choked out the words.

Jack hung his head and left Rominger to his privacy.

Dr. Reynolds injected the final shot to the dog.

"It's okay...sleep now... sleep..."

Major's breathing slowed and then finally stopped as Rominger continued to speak softly and pet him.

In the parking lot, Deputy McPherson drove up and parked. He quickly met up with Jack at the back of the hospital. "How's Major?" he asked breathlessly.

Jack shook his head. "No."

"No… no… no…" McPherson sighed.

Jack changed the subject. "Did you see a black SUV leave here?"

"No, why?"

"They were concerned citizens who helped get us here. I guess they left. We didn't get to thank them." Jack was still wracking his brain to where he might have seen them before.

A black BMW drove into the parking lot and parked. A pretty blonde woman got out and saw Jack.

Deputy McPherson interrupted. "Maybe you should—?"

"I'm fine," Jack snapped.

The woman approached and said simply, "Jack." Her eyes were teary; obviously the bad news traveled fast.

"Tara…Blake's going to really need you now," Jack said with some compassion but little inflection.

Tara hesitated as if about to say something, but instead looked down at the ground and went inside to be with Blake.

Deputy McPherson tried to lighten the situation. "You must really be over her."

"Yeah." Jack glanced at the examination room. "Who's got Keno?"

"Sullivan."

Both officers went to McPherson's cruiser, where a large German shepherd wagged his tail.

"Make sure you give Booker a big treat tonight." Jack smiled, but his eyes were deeply sad as he got into the passenger side of the police car.

"You bet," McPherson answered. "And a big drink for me—maybe two or more."

CHAPTER THIRTY-SEVEN

Deputy McPherson pulled up to where Jack's cruiser waited. Sullivan waved as he left Jack's patrol car for him and approached his own. There was a tow truck slowly towing away Darrell's parked black Honda.

Detective Sergeant Martinez was directing a crime scene tech around the car and consulting on possible evidence.

Jack and McPherson approached the detective.

There was an alert on the detective's phone. He immediately pushed a few buttons and examined what he saw.

"What the—?" He saw several photos of the parked cars around the crime scene and photos of the drivers. It showed the photo of Darrell inside the Honda. The text and email came from an unknown source.

"What's up?" Jack asked. He was curious about the car because he had remembered seeing it when he'd arrived at the hostage situation.

The detective explained, "Looks like we found a stolen car and the several descriptions of the person driving it seem to match one of our county's most wanted. Here's a photo that was emailed to me." He showed his phone to the deputies.

"Which one?" Deputy McPherson asked, raising his eyebrows.

"It looks like the photo is Monty Stinger who has four aliases. It also fits his MO for stealing cars."

"Darrell Brooks?" Jack's gut began to work overtime.

"Yeah, and we have three last possible known locations of residency to check out." The detective

186

watched Jack's reaction. "The car is wrapped up tight for forensics to go over too."

"Who's checking out the addresses?" Jack said quickly.

The detective referred to his small notepad. "Detectives Preston and Turner are checking out a small low income apartment in south Salinas…two patrolmen are over at the Cozy Inn by the Bay in Castroville…and—"

"And?" Jack pressed.

The detective smiled at both eager-faced deputies. "Thought I could use a couple of K9 units to check out an apartment in Monterey with me." He tore off a piece of paper with the address and handed it to Jack.

"Let's roll," Jack replied.

* * * * *

Two young patrol deputies followed a disheveled, overweight motel manager in his early sixties to Darrell's rented room at the Cozy Inn by the Bay. There wasn't anything cozy about it. The place was actually seedy and uninviting. Most residents in the county never even noticed it or ever heard of the name of the small motel.

The manager with shaky hands and bad breath unlocked the door with his passkey. Swiftly, both deputies entered the room and found it empty. Clothes and fast food wrappers covered the table and two mismatched chairs. The deputies continued to search the closet and bathroom, but there wasn't anything useful.

Darrell wasn't there.

The motel manager offered, "He pretty much kept to himself, but I knew that there was something not quite right about him. Those eyes, ya know—"

"When was the last time you saw him?" the shorter deputy asked, still looking at the garbage around the room.

"Oh, this morning…early…left in a dark Honda car, I think…"

* * * * *

Blood drops and smears covered the old, discolored linoleum bathroom floor. The drag marks looked like they were from both directions in and out of the bathroom. Part of the blood had dried in crusty spots, while in other places, the blood was still fresh and vibrant.

Tad exited the bathroom carrying two large garbage bags. His clothes were soaked in his brother's blood and his own heavy, dripping perspiration. He absently wiped his forehead. He didn't count on the fact that it was going to be like a hard day of work to dismember one body.

The bathtub showed only the grisly residues of blood, bone, and cartilage along with the cast offs from the hacksaw. There was one smaller bag on the vanity that contained Darrell's head wrapped in double plastic to keep anything from leaking out.

Tad took a quick bath from the kitchen sink and wiped up any remaining blood spatter. He calmly changed his shirt and pants, leaving evidence on the apartment floor next to the bagged remains of Darrell.

* * * * *

Detectives Preston and Turner arrived at the Salinas apartment complex with a uniformed deputy. They walked through the main entrance to find apartment 29. After a quick assessment, they went around to the south side and up a staircase. It appeared to be the only way in and out.

Turner instructed the deputy, "Wait here in case he makes us."

The detectives jogged up the stairs toward apartment 29. They pulled their service weapons as they stood at the threshold of the apartment, each taking a position on opposite sides of the door. They gave each other the eye and nod, meaning that they were each good to go and ready for anything.

Preston hammered on the door. "Sheriff's office! Open the door!"

No sounds.

No movement from inside.

"Police! Open up!" she demanded.

Quiet.

Preston shifted her weight slightly and moved farther away from the door to give her partner room to move.

Turner took a step back from the door and gave a stomp kick with his right foot. The flimsy door slammed opened easily with only a few splintered remnants left behind.

Both detectives rushed into the apartment, clearing each room as they went. They met in the middle of the living room.

"Damn!" Turner looked around. "It looks like no one has been here in a while."

The apartment only had two empty beer cans on the floor next to a tattered, broken-down yellow sofa.

CHAPTER THIRTY-EIGHT

An unmarked Ford Taurus and two K9 police cruisers made their way to the apartment location in Monterey. They drove at a steady speed, careful of meandering pedestrians and other motorists pulling out from driveways and parking lots.

Deputy McPherson tried to keep up with the two other vehicles, but a civilian truck got in front of him. Suddenly, a middle-aged woman with short black hair jumped out in the street to flag him down.

He slammed on his brakes, barely missing her as she ran up to his window.

Clearly distressed, she begged Deputy McPherson for help. "Please help us! We've just been robbed and they had a gun!"

The deputy pulled to the side of the road and watched Jack and the Detective Sergeant Martinez speed away to the apartment. He was a little disappointed, but he also had an important job of helping the citizens. He called in his current position and the reporting party complaint.

* * * * *

Tad easily tossed the last garbage bags inside the dumpster and shut the top. He knew that trash pickup would be the next morning, so he wouldn't have to worry about any stench that would bring suspicion and then the cops.

He was already gone before Jack and the detective arrived, but they only missed each other by minutes at the dumpster.

* * * * *

Jack parked away from the main entrance of the apartment complex not to raise suspicion or be seen before he wanted to be seen. He didn't see where the detective parked, but assumed that he too was worried about alerting Darrell Brooks of their visit.

Jack opened the back door and Keno was ready for some serious action.

Detective Sergeant Martinez met up with Jack at his car. "The entrance is on the outside—eastside. You and Keno go around and come up the back way to meet me."

"Do we wait for McPherson or backup?"

"No," Martinez said flatly.

Jack was excited that he might be a part of arresting one of the most wanted criminals in the area. "We're on it."

Jack and Keno took off and jogged away from the detective around the small, neglected apartment compound. There didn't seem to be anyone around, which was good due to the problems that nosey neighbors would contribute to their arrest.

Jack and Keno moved around the building, keeping a watchful eye for anything that was suspicious or out of place.

Keno stopped and sat next to a garbage dumpster.

"C'mon, Keno," Jack urged. He was a little annoyed by the dog's behavior.

Keno stayed and whined. He walked to the dumpster and began clawing with his large front paws.

Jack decided to investigate. He slowly opened the dumpster lid. The reek of death immediately hit him. There were several black plastic garbage bags. He decided to tear a small hole in the smaller one. His sardonic side hoped that it was just a dead pet cat, hamster, or bird that had attracted Keno to the spot.

As Jack began to tear away the plastic, he found what seemed to be several layers of clear, heavy plastic underneath. He kept tearing. The small opening revealed the dead eyes of Darrell Brooks staring straight at him. Instinctively, he jumped back, repulsed but relieved that he was dead. At least the courts wouldn't have to waste their time on this criminal.

"Good boy, Keno," Jack said as he raised his hand to his nose to keep the stench away.

He carefully closed the lid, making sure that he only touched the dumpster in the same place. Forensics would have to process the dumpster and the apartment. He wanted to give the detective the news personally and not over the radio.

"Let's go, Keno."

Jack and Keno hurried around the building to meet up with Martinez.

* * * * *

The detective had already made his way to the apartment. He moved slowly, with caution. The front door was slightly open—either someone forgot to close it or they were planning on coming right back outside. He scathed the exterior wall with his Glock aimed in front of him, ready for Darrell Brooks to make his escape.

He edged even closer and peered inside through the cracked door. He could see a duffle bag sitting a few feet inside, slightly opened, and it disclosed weapons and ammunition.

There was no one in sight, but they had to be only a few feet from the door. He knew that he had the guy they had been hunting for.

The detective smiled slyly to himself.

Your time on the outside is over.

He glanced back to where he came from and there was no one in sight. He wondered where Jack and Keno were. He continued to wait to enter the apartment and thought he might have to ambush Darrell Brooks when he came out.

As the detective looked back inside the apartment, something shiny caught his eye for an instant.

A deafening gun blast shattered straight through the hollow door and slammed into the detective. He was pushed back into the banister and knocked completely off his feet. His left shoulder and chest took a direct hit. The detective sergeant laid on his back barely conscious and bleeding. His semi-conscious mind wavered in and out of reality from the pressure and intense pain.

Tad exited the apartment and ran full speed down the stairs carrying the duffle bag. He disappeared.

Within seconds, Jack and Keno rounded the back corner behind the apartment. "Martinez!" With gun drawn, Jack quickly scanned the area for the perp.

Once satisfied, he dropped to his knees at the detective's side and checked for a pulse.

Keno barked persistently in the direction of Tad's bold escape.

Martinez weakly said, "Go after him...the vest took most of the hit."

Jack quickly radioed into dispatch. "Shots fired...officer down at 5887 4th Avenue, Apartment 17. Request back up and ambulance."

"Dammit, Jack! Go!" the detective insisted with a raspy tone.

Deputy McPherson jogged up the stairs and had a sick look on his face when he saw the detective lying on the ground. "Oh, God." He dropped down and helped to stop the bleeding.

The detective was getting angry now. "Go, Jack! Go after him! Don't let him get away…"

Jack knew there was nothing he could do at the scene but wait for help to arrive. He needed to go after him. He didn't have time to explain that Darrell Brooks was cut up in small pieces in the dumpster and that the man who'd just shot the detective was Tad Brooks. This man was supposedly dead, but magically had come back to life. All of these thoughts ran through his mind in record time.

He stood up and said to McPherson, "Stay with him!"

Jack and Keno ran down the stairs before anyone could say anything.

McPherson yelled after him. "Jack! Wait for backup!"

CHAPTER THIRTY-NINE

Three police cars, an ambulance, and a fire truck stopped in front of the apartment building. There were more sirens wailing in the distance. People were beginning to appear outside their homes to see what all the commotion was about.

A block away, Jack gave Keno several extra feet of lead. He did not have time to get the long tracking lead or Keno's harness. Keno had picked up a track of Tad's scent. It appeared that the suspect didn't get into a getaway car, so that meant he was close and didn't have time to put some serious distance between himself and the cops.

There were several warehouses that had been vacated and tenants had gone out of business. They were in the process of renovating the buildings instead of tearing them down and rebuilding. One particular run down warehouse had been boarded up and half the windows were broken out, leaving jagged pieces of glass scattered on the ground.

Jack recalled that one of the warehouses had been the crime scene for one of the serial killer victims, a young girl who had been brutally stabbed and found inside a large toolbox.

A piece of yellow crime scene tape fluttered by and Jack quickly scanned the buildings and saw that one next to it was the crime scene, still with some tape stretched across the doorway.

Jack brought his attention back to the abandoned warehouse.

Keno kept his muzzle to the ground and momentarily hesitated. He located a familiar scent and it was strong. Jack unsnapped the dog's lead.

"Keno, search."

Panting and clearly ready for work, Keno padded around the building to a flapping board recently pried away from the old back doorway. He pawed at the makeshift wood entrance.

Jack knew that he had the suspect trapped like a rat. "Down," he ordered.

The dog obediently downed and waited for the next command.

He reported to dispatch. "Deputy Davis needs assistance of fleeing, armed suspect at..." He looked around to get an exact location. "Third warehouse on Second Street. Please advise."

There were loud static sounds on his radio.

Jack repeated his request.

A muddled voice responded.

He wasn't sure if they had heard his request or not.

Keno stood up and began to bark. The dog took two steps and clawed furiously at the old entrance. He squeezed his muscular body through the outlet and disappeared inside the building.

"Keno, come! Keno!" Jack was worried that Keno would be face-to-face with an armed suspect and there would be another K9 fatality. He pulled back the loose opening and squeezed his body through. His awkward utility belt cost him a few extra seconds.

Inside the dark warehouse, Jack clicked on his small flashlight and proceeded with caution. He had his gun drawn and could feel goose bumps form on his arms and the back of his neck—cop instinct amped up in high gear.

The interior was heavy with dust and cobwebs. The air was thick and moldy. There was an old rickety scaffolding, unused lumber, plastic utility buckets, paint cans, and two large storage containers. Everything had been abandoned and just left where the last workers had left them. It was strange to see that a construction job had been abandoned and no one had bothered to come back and pick up the supplies and tools.

"Keno, come," he softly said.

He looked up and saw Keno crawling up a ladder two stories high that led across a skywalk. His shiny black coat glistened in the low light.

"Keno!" He kept an eye out for the suspect. He thought perhaps the perp had escaped out another entrance or window.

The dog stopped and waited, but didn't down. He began to pant heavily.

"Keno, down. Stay!" Jack didn't want the dog to take a fall because there were too many things in the warehouse that would cause serious injury if he fell on them.

Jack hurried up to Keno's location. Just as he reached the dog, gunshots ricocheted off the scaffolding and circuit breakers, causing sparks to fly around wildly. Instinctively, Jack grabbed the scruff of Keno's large neck and they both slid down a ladder, landing hard behind large sheets of wood and steel bars.

Taking cover and shielding Keno, Jack returned fire. His rounds barely made an impact compared to the blasting from the large caliber military rounds that were exploding all around them.

"You can't escape!" Jack yelled. He heard his voice in an eerie echo.

"Who says I want to?" Tad said, moving to a far corner away from Jack's view.

Jack and Keno moved through the warehouse toward the sound of Tad's voice, taking cover at every possible opportunity.

Keno stayed on his belly and crawled along with his partner.

Several fifty and hundred-pound cement bags fell all around them from above, leaving a white smoky powder in the air. Jack stifled a cough and concentrated on keeping his bearings in the warehouse through the heavy white cloud.

The room had almost a funhouse effect on his perception. He knew that they had to get out. There was that inner cop voice urging him to do so right now—immediately.

Jack was just about to round another corner when he saw Tad fishing more ammunition out of his duffle bag.

He retreated. Jack dared not to make a sound or breathe. He used hand signals to make Keno down and stay before he proceeded.

The dog obeyed.

Jack saw his opportunity and took it. He surprised Tad by confronting him with his gun targeted at his head. "Stand up and put your hands on your head! Now!"

Tad hesitated.

"Do it now!"

Tad turned his body slightly and tossed a grenade from his right hand.

JENNIFER CHASE

Both Jack and Tad dove in different directions for cover as the grenade exploded, causing a rushing avalanche of lumber and steel to tumble down.

Thick dust clouds immediately sucked up the oxygen.

Jack hit the hard cement floor and rolled to avoid being hit by any of the falling debris. His gun bounced out of sight. He slowly sat up, dazed by the loud noise and his vision was blurry. Everything buzzed in his ears and the only thing he could hear was his rapid heartbeat. His wits began to gather and he realized Keno wasn't at his side. "Keno," he uttered with a sick, nauseating feeling in his stomach.

The huge pile of rubble almost six feet high completely covered the areas where the dog had obediently waited for his partner's next command. His rage grew like he had never felt it before. He wanted blood and revenge for what this dreg of society had done to all of his victims and his dog.

Jack could see Tad lying face down.

Jack slowly got to his feet and staggered a few steps over to Tad. He grabbed Tad's shirt and forcefully rolled him over to see his eyes were closed and several wounds on his forehead were bleeding. If Tad wasn't already dead, Jack was going to make sure that he was shortly.

"You sonofabitch!" he screamed. Yelling actually made his head pulsate and he became lightheaded.

Tad grabbed Jack's wrist with such a twisting force it made his knees buckle to the ground. They scrambled, each trying desperately to get the upper hand. Neither had anything to lose, by their own calculations.

More falling debris showered all around them. The blast had made the building unstable and it was obvious

199

that it could bury them at any moment. The building creaked and groaned. Glass continued to break and shower down to the floor.

Ted pounded Jack with his fists. It was clear that the killer had boxed before and in combination with rage, he made a deadly opponent. He then spun and expertly gave Jack a roundhouse kick to the ribs, sending him through an unfinished wall. Drywall and splintered two by fours were left in his path.

Jack felt like he had been beaten by Mike Tyson and then thrown out of a speeding truck. He was dazed and trying to catch his breath. There was a searing pain in his ribs every time he inhaled. He rolled over onto his side and could see that Tad was winding up to bash his brains in with a four foot steel bar.

Tad let out a savage rebel yell as he began to gain momentum for the fatal swing at Jack. His eyes were crazed and it was clear that he wanted blood, guts, and death.

A black blur of paws and white teeth glided through the air. With the equal force of a bomb falling from the sky, Keno hit Tad like a linebacker and clamped down on his shoulder, taking him directly to the ground and causing him to drop the steel bar on impact.

Keno took several savage bites with his massive jaw as Tad tried to shield himself from the attack.

"Keno, off!" Jack was relieved, but still worried that the dog's injuries could be made worse by fighting with Tad.

The dog retreated, staggering to one side and collapsed. Blood rolled down his once shiny beautiful coat. He panted rapidly.

Tad scurried the best he could to get to some of his deadly weapons.

Jack had other ideas for Tad and he wanted to be the one to have the last word. He picked up the metal bar with every ounce of strength he had and skewered Tad through the torso.

It was easier than he first had thought and he hoped it hit a couple of major organs.

Tad tried to roll over with the complete look of surprise on his face, but the long steel bar wouldn't let him. He slowly surrendered to a painful death.

Jack dropped to the ground, thinking he could walk no farther.

Keno crawled over to him, bleeding from his head and upper shoulder. He laid his head and paw on Jack's lap.

The warehouse made a long, agonizing groan that sounded more like a plea for help.

Jack knew that he couldn't crawl out to safety and he was going to die under the weight of the falling building. He petted Keno and so many memories flooded him, even childhood memories of going fishing and when he'd graduated from the police academy. Good memories and he knew that if he had everything to do over again, he wouldn't have changed a thing about his life.

A calm peace washed over him.

The building started to rumble and it sounded like a major earthquake from above and not from the earth. Walls were starting to crumble and fragments of the building began to shower down hard.

Jack closed his eyes and waited for the inevitable.

He felt a slight graze across his right arm and then a firmer tug helping him to his feet. Two people had braved the falling building in order to save him and Keno. He blinked several times expecting to see cops or fireman uniforms, but instead, it was a man and woman dressed in civilian clothing.

The woman held Jack by the waist and allowed him to lean on her as they made their way to the exit. The door was open wide and he could see the daylight and remembered what a clear, sunny day it had been.

A dark-haired, muscular man carried Keno out to safety.

The group barely made it through the entrance—before the final collapse.

Jack caught his breath, coughing violently every few seconds. His face and ribs were killing him. He turned and watched the building disintegrate into itself. The momentum carried the structure down like dominos.

For the first time, he looked at his rescuers and recognized the striking couple from the Chinese restaurant and the ride to the veterinary emergency hospital. He wasn't sure, but he had seen them in several other places too.

Police cars were approaching fast.

The couple smiled at Jack; there was also some relief seeing he was alive, and then they disappeared down the street away from the oncoming emergency vehicles.

Jack croaked. "Hey, wait. Who are you?" He knew that he'd probably never know, but thanked God that they were around to save him and Keno from a terrible fate. They were their guardian angels.

Jack looked down and saw that Keno wasn't moving. He moved next to the big dog and pulled him close on his lap as he began to cry.

Several police cars and two fire trucks arrived while more were on their way.

CHAPTER FORTY

The sun was shining brightly and accentuated the impeccable police uniforms. Hundreds of police officers and civilians attended the K9 funeral. It was a dazzling spectacle with a line of more than two dozen standing K9 officers and their sitting, four-legged partners that positioned themselves straight ahead.

At the front of the line, Keno's black coat shined in the sun, even with the large white bandage on his left leg along with several stitches on his shoulder and floppy right ear. He sat proudly next to Jack with a badge of honor he'd been given by the sheriff for his bravery in apprehending a wanted felon. He was the only Labrador Retriever in the impressive line of working German shepherds, Malinois, and Rottweilers.

Jack was feeling better with only one broken rib and numerous cuts and abrasions. He felt that he was the lucky one. He looked over to Deputy Rominger, who remained like a statue standing with Tara at his side. He wore the pain he felt on his handsome, well-chiseled face.

Sergeant Weaver took up a position next to the small casket in order to give a speech. He slowly began, "A police officer's job involves risks and challenges that we cannot always understand, even though we're trained for tragedy and loss of life." He looked through the crowd. "A K9 officer has to be ready for all of those things except losing a K9 partner…"

CHAPTER FORTY-ONE

The hospital room was decorated with colorful get-well cards, balloons, and funny looking stuffed animals dressed in police uniforms. Propped up in a hospital bed and still hooked up to fluids was Detective Sergeant Martinez.

Several file folders were neatly stacked on the side table. It was obvious that he was working on cases, not just closing them.

Jack entered the room with a box of cigars. "You up for a visitor?" He smiled.

"Not unless you're going to break me out of here," Martinez said with little cheer.

"Sick of the joint already?" Jack was so relieved that he was okay and that the bulletproof vest had taken most of the force. There were still bullet fragments that penetrated his shoulder, but he was expected to make a full recovery.

"I guess I should be thankful I'm still alive. He could've blown my head off instead." Martinez smiled a little.

Jack gave him the box of cigars. "Here's something that will guarantee to shorten your life."

"Thanks."

Jack looked around and could barely tell that it was a hospital room with all of the decorations. "Didn't think you needed any more cheery balloons."

"I mean for taking my shooter out." He kept Jack's gaze.

"I'm just sorry that I wasn't there sooner." Jack meant it, but he almost hadn't made it out of the warehouse. If he had been there sooner, things would have turned out differently. He turned to leave. "You take it easy. The department's not the same without you, even though you closed the case on a serial killer."

"Jack?" Martinez said softly. Something weighed heavy on him.

"Yeah."

"There were two killers."

"What?" Jack couldn't believe what he had heard. "What do you mean?"

The detective hated what he had to tell Jack, but it was obvious that no one had talked to him yet. "Did Megan come with you?"

"She's out waiting in the hall." He had a bad feeling. Call it a cop's instinct. "Why?"

The detective grimaced as he leaned over to pick up two official-looking file folders. "I wanted to tell you first."

"What are you talking about?" Jack had the sudden urge to flee the hospital and keep on running.

"The three butcher knives taken from Megan's kitchen," he began slowly. "One was found in Brooks' car and the other two were used to kill two other people. All three knives are accounted for."

Jack walked closer to the bed. "What are you saying?"

"Jack..." he hesitated. "The three knives that were used to kill the two prostitutes and Megan's sister were both found with Megan's fingerprints on them." He watched for his friend's reaction, but there was none. "A forensic tech found one of the knives in a storm drain and the others weren't difficult to find as they were close to the crime scenes."

"What do you mean?" It was all that Jack could say as he began to run scenarios through his mind.

"All three knives were bought from a specialty knife store and the sales person remembered Megan buying them. Brooks didn't kill Teresa."

"Why are you doing this?" he managed to whisper.

The detective took a deep breath. "Jack, it's the truth."

Jack took a step back and was unable to say a word, but he knew that the evidence—or the detective, for that matter—didn't lie.

He hurried out of the room.

"Jack… Jack…" The detective sighed and leaned back against his pillows.

* * * * *

Jack walked down the hallway to where Megan was sitting reading a magazine. She looked up when she saw him approach with urgency and stood up.

"Is Detective Martinez okay?" She looked worried.

"Why?" Jack could barely speak.

"What?"

"Why after all this time did you come back into my life?" He took a step back because he was afraid of what he might do if he let his anger explode. "Was I your perfect alibi?"

"Jack, what are you talking about?" she said as her eyes searched his.

He grabbed her by the shoulders.

"You're hurting me. What's wrong?" she asked, seeing the rage in his eyes.

"It's like you made me an accomplice." He squeezed her arms harder. "I loved you." He moved away from her. "Why?" He wanted an answer no matter what it was going to be.

Megan's eyes filled with tears. She couldn't keep her secret anymore. As she crumbled emotionally, her legs folded and she dropped to the floor. She pushed herself back against the wall, pulled her knees up to her body, and began to chant to herself.

Jack could only watch her.

She was like a stranger and not the woman he had loved. Her face was clouded and confused as she twisted against her body's structure. It was like watching someone in solitary confinement suffer from within their own mind.

Megan began to explain in her feeble way, "Jack, you know how I feel about you, you *have* to understand."

"Don't!" Jack yelled.

She continued to stare at the floor. "You don't understand! You don't understand…"

Her words faded away in the hospital hallway as she remembered all of the graphic details… she only wanted to be at peace now.

* * * * *

The compulsive feeling overwhelmed her as she didn't have the will to stop herself. The air around her in the warehouse felt claustrophobic but comforting at the same time. If she closed her eyes, the sheer momentum would carry her to complete the task. There was no other choice for what she had to do—needed to do.

The knife felt good in her hand. It was solid, firm, and had a unique energy which propelled her.

The toolbox was closed and it seemed to antagonize her, daring her to do it. Megan flipped open the box and saw the young girl inside. Her eyes were crazed and terrified beyond anything that she could have imagined. She watched the girl try to wiggle out of her restraints, but it was no use.

With a deep breath, Megan raised the knife and plunged it deep into the girl's stomach. The girl stopped moving and her eyes seemed to glaze over. It felt good to Megan as she stabbed the girl numerous more times. Elated, she felt she was safe once again. It was like she was watching herself die and she would then finally be able to have peace in her life.

* * * * *

Megan stood in the kitchen with the dog food bowl in front of her on the counter. She stared at it for some time before she opened the cupboard under the sink and took out rat poison. As if in a trance, she shook out some of the powdered poison.

Everything good, innocent, and loyal was a part of the domestic canine.

She wanted so much to gain back her innocence and have life to live over again. Maybe she could have saved her mother's life. It was possible that things could have been different. Maybe her mother could have taken her and Teresa and gone far away.

They would have been safe and happy.

She couldn't help but want to extinguish everything that was good and innocent before something terrible happened. It was the only way that she could survive and possibly have the chance to begin again. She was driven to do what she was going to do. She picked up the bowl and set it on the floor.

* * * * *

Megan recalled the chain of events during that horrific night in her home. She had opened her bedroom door slightly and peered through the tiny crack, then shut the door quietly.

In her bedroom, Teresa slept peacefully on her back with the comforter neatly folded under her arms. A knife rose and plunged into her chest. She abruptly awoke with a strangled scream.

She saw Megan standing over her with the knife held high.

With a gurgled whimper, she said. "Why?" She tried to protect herself from the next blow.

In the struggle, the phone and a couple of books were knocked off the nightstand. Teresa flopped onto the floor, trying desperately to crawl to safety.

Megan raised the knife again and thrust it through Teresa's back repeatedly.

* * * * *

As Megan caught her breath outside the Chinese restaurant, she felt a familiar confidence fill her body. She knew what she must do. She heard a couple of voices around the corner and then it was quiet. As she made her way to the end of the alley and turned the corner, she saw a young girl who had obviously been working and exchanging sex for money any way she could.

Megan walked up to her and smiled.

The girl smiled back, unsure, and asked, "You're not looking for a date, are you?" She eyed Megan curiously.

Megan's well-rehearsed movements made the girl nervous.

Megan slipped her hand in her purse and could feel the blade against her slender fingers. She moved her nails over the two edges and could feel it slightly cut them. This excited her because she did not want the heightened feeling to end.

Her life would then be normal again.

"Are you lost?" the girl asked.

Megan smiled and confronted her. "No." She withdrew the knife and sliced the girl across the carotid artery. Blood gushed from the girl's neck as Megan stepped to one side to miss the spurting fluid.

She watched the girl try to stop the bleeding, but it was pointless. She slowly fell to the ground.

* * * * *

Two security guards helped Megan up, but when she realized what was going on she began to scream and fight with every ounce of energy she had.

Jack watched, unable to move. He recalled the events from the past couple of weeks and he still couldn't believe any of it.

Megan contorted her body as she continued to scream apologies and profanity.

Everything was a lie.

Nothing was real.

Heartbroken and devastated, Jack watched them take Megan away.

Still fuming, she yelled obscenities of death at anyone who listened about how all she had ever wanted was peace and innocence back.

CHAPTER FORTY-TWO

Birds fluttered from tree to tree as the sun cascaded through the branches. The grass had been recently cut and neatly trimmed around the edges.

Two benches faced the small pond and looked inviting for any visitor to take a moment to gaze at the scenery or take a rest. The view was picture perfect, but not for those who were only allowed to view it through a window. They wouldn't feel the warmth of the sun or the light breeze upon their face.

Megan sat in a white wicker chair, staring aimlessly out the window at the beautiful park setting. Trapped in the prison of her own mind, the beauty was lost on her. Reality didn't have a place with her anymore.

A young nurse with dark hair pulled back in a ponytail tucked a small quilt around her. "Megan, it's time to take your medicine," she announced. The nurse put two white pills directly into Megan's mouth, gently closed her jaw, and then offered her a glass of water.

Megan remained unresponsive and continued to stare out the window. Her mind was forever playing repeatedly the events of her life from when she was a child through her killing spree on an endless loop of despair, terror, and death.

* * * * *

The brilliant sun sparkled on the bay as seagulls flew overhead. Except for a few joggers, the beach was almost deserted. Waves lapped up against the shoreline, wetting the pristine sand. Two sailboats took the opportunity to enjoy the perfect breeze and moved along the horizon at a leisurely pace.

A football soared through the air. It landed down the shoreline and tumbled several times in the shallow water.

Keno hustled at full speed and grabbed the Nerf football in his strong jaw. He didn't miss the moment to prance from side to side with his prize before returning to Jack. His black, sleek coat shined in the sun from the reflection of the water. His bandages were gone, but the scars would be evident for some time.

Jack whistled to his partner. "Good boy." He called out and waited for the dog to return.

Tina ran circles around Jack and then dashed down the shore to greet Keno. Her golden fur contrasted the coal black coat of Keno.

Keno finally dropped the wet ball in front of Jack, eagerly waiting for it to rocket down the beach again. His tongue hung out on the left side of his jaw and he appeared to be smiling.

It made Jack smile.

He grabbed the football and took a couple of steps, mimicking his best quarterback stance before releasing the ball.

Keno jumped up and down begging for the ball to go even farther this time. Jack threw the ball with most of his strength and it caught a tailwind.

Jack watched the wave set coming in and couldn't help but think that every wave opened up a potential for a new beginning. Many things weighed heavily on his mind, but for now, each day was getting better and would continue to do so. Wounds healed, both physical and emotional, but things would be bright and would flourish once again. It was all that he could hope for in his life.

SILENT PARTNER

THE END

CPSIA information can be obtained
at www.ICGtesting.com
Printed in the USA
FSHW011358150121
77605FS